Reprise

Reprise

Lela Gilbert

WORD PUBLISHING
Dallas•London•Vancouver•Melbourne

This novel is a work of fiction. Names, characters, places, and incidents are either the product of the author's imagination or are used fictitiously. Any resemblance to actual events, locales, organizations, or persons, living or dead, is entirely coincidental and beyond the intent of either the author or the publisher.

All Scripture quotations, unless otherwise noted, are from the Holy Bible, New International Version. Copyright © 1973, 1978, 1984 International Bible Society. Used by permission of Zondervan Bible Publishers.

Library of Congress Cataloging-in-Publication Data:

Gilbert, Lela.
    Reprise / Lela Gilbert.
      p. cm.
      ISBN 0-8499-3482-6 (Trade paper)
      ISBN 0-8499-3878-3 (Mass paper)
      I. Title.
    PS3557.I34223R46 1993
    813' .54—dc20   93-22516
                                                              CIP

Printed in the United States of America

56789 OPM 987654321

For Dylan and Colin.

1

For our fears, give us courage
In our tears, find a song.
For our doubts, grant conviction,
Where we're weak, make us strong.
Turn our faults into blessings,
Turn our griefs into praise.
And for dark hours of sadness
Give us bright, golden days.

Elisabeth Surrey-Dixon's crown of blonde hair gleamed among the many candles, and her smile outshone every light in the room. The words her new husband Jon Surrey-Dixon had just read were those of a simple verse she had written—a verse that captured her dearest vision for their future together. Apparently it reflected Jon's dreams too, because he had framed it, along with a portrait he had taken of Elisabeth with his best camera, and had given it to her as her wedding present.

In the splendor of the moment, the poem was both touching and appropriate. To look beyond the immediate romance of the wedding would have seemed cynical, even to the most hardened observer, and the thought of the verse being prescient or even prophetic never crossed the mind of any of the wedding guests. Everyone had chosen to forget the unpleasantries that had marred the past of both the bride and the groom. If they came to mind at all, they were assumed dead, buried, and about to be resurrected as blessings in the garden of perpetual marital bliss.

Jon Surrey-Dixon—professional photographer, former hostage, and bridegroom—had finally found his way to the altar with Elisabeth Casey—former model and writer of books, affectionately known to him as Betty. The two of them had survived a nightmarish year of separation, courtesy of the Lebanese Islamic Jihad. Hoping for a hefty ransom, Middle Eastern terrorists had kidnapped Jon and held him, blindfolded and bloodied, in Beirut. The tragedy had begun just four days before their original wedding date.

Betty had waited for Jon through months of uncertainty and emotional distress. Now, at last, her faith in his ultimate deliverance and return to her waiting arms had been rewarded. Now, on a flawless spring day, the long-postponed wedding had unfolded perfectly. And now, having read Betty's poem aloud at the reception, Jon kissed the bride on her forehead and lifted his glass to the guests.

"One last toast," he smiled, his eyes bright with happiness. "Or maybe I should say one last prayer. Here's to all of you who stood with Betty throughout my captivity. May God reward every one of you for your kindness to her—and to me. We will never forget you and all you've done for us."

Jon's words were received with quiet smiles and a murmur of assent. Everyone knew that it had been an agonizing year for both of them. Jon had been beaten and locked up, deprived of food and comfort, with little hope of survival. Betty had been left at the mercy of the media, an odd assortment of opportunists, and the ever-aloof U.S. State Department. A few such recollections seemed to remind the wedding guests that it was a miracle the nuptials had ever come about at all. Jon's sobering words also seemed to announce the end of the reception.

Standing at Jon's side, Betty was the personification of joy, hope, and optimism. Bedecked in ice-blue silk and pearls, she simply couldn't stop smiling even when she tried. Again and again, she and Jon hugged and kissed their friends, loved ones, and relatives. They also persistently refused to answer any inquiries about their honeymoon. Although they had originally planned a trip to London, an unexpected wedding gift from Betty's father, Harold Fuller, had given them second thoughts. Harold had generously provided airline tickets to Hawaii.

"It just sounds so peaceful," Betty said to Jon as they were gathering the last of the presents. "After weeks of getting ready for all this, I feel like lying in the sun, listening to the ocean, and accomplishing absolutely nothing for a while. What do you think? I want you to decide."

Jon hardly hesitated. "We'd be doing a lot of running around and sightseeing in London instead of relaxing, wouldn't we? We'll have the London tickets, so we can use them later. I'm with you. I think I'd rather relax. Let's go to Hawaii."

"Of course I'll have to buy a new wardrobe . . ." Betty's eyes narrowed as she glanced at Jon for a possible reaction.

"That's okay," he smiled, a bit patronizing. "All you'll need is a bottle of sun screen and a bathing suit. That shouldn't be too expensive."

"What about shorts? Tank tops? T-shirts? And a little something for those romantic tropical evenings?"

"Like I said, a bathing suit and sun screen. I guess you might want to take along a sun dress," he added benevolently.

Men! Betty shook her head as she collected several identical glass salad bowls and repacked them in the appropriate white gift box. She mentally inventoried her wardrobe. Whatever got her through the hottest California summers would probably be useful in Hawaii. She could use the more citified items she'd bought for London later on.

And so, two days later, Mr. and Mrs. Jon Surrey-Dixon boarded a United Airlines 747, buckled themselves into their seats, and began their first adventure as husband and wife.

A quick survey of the plane revealed an array of colorful shirts stretched across bulging middle-aged midriffs. "What do you think we'll be doing when we're that old?" Betty poked Jon in the ribs, distracting him from his *Modern Photography* magazine. She pointed toward a well-heeled, fiftysomething couple across the aisle, holding hands as they slept beneath matching airline blankets.

"Whatever we're doing, we'll be doing it together. That much I know for sure." Jon dismissed Betty by kissing her on the nose. He then returned his attention to an apparently fascinating article. From what Betty could gather, peering over his shoulder, it was an in-depth discourse about camera apertures.

She glanced out the window and down at the Pacific Ocean, sparkling thirty-five thousand feet beneath them. Her thoughts were as calm as the sea. A warming sense of reality arose within her. She was *really* here, *really* sitting beside the man of her dreams, *really* married to him, *really* starting a brand-new life with him. She studied his now-familiar profile, a quiet smile playing around her mouth. His angular face was relaxed; his intelligent eyes as blue as the sun-spangled sea below.

Reflection carried her back across the years. Her first marriage had lacked feeling; it was almost mechanical. How could she have thought she had loved Carlton? Jon was so much a part of her, so much in tune with her. He was like her "other half." In retrospect, Carlton seemed like a cardboard cutout of a person—nothing but facade. She shook her head in disbelief. *How could I have married Carlton? What was wrong with me?*

"What?" Jon looked up. "Why are you shaking your head? What have I done?" He closed his magazine in mock contrition.

Betty was caught off guard. "Oh I was just thinking about . . . oh, nothing Jon."

"What? Now I'm curious."

"Oh, I was just thinking about my first marriage and about Carlton. I just can't believe I married a man I hardly knew!"

Jon studied her face for a moment. His eyes narrowed. "You aren't drawing any unfavorable comparisons between him and me, are you?"

"Only unfavorable to him, Jon. Not to worry."

He smirked and shrugged. Reopening the magazine, he soon became engrossed in a colorful chart detailing pertinent facts about film, light, and lens speed.

I wonder what his early days with Carla were like. An uncomfortable emotion rippled through Betty. Jon rarely mentioned his first wife. In all the time she'd known him, he had said very little about his feelings for her. Betty knew almost nothing about their relationship, except that Jon had been deeply disappointed in it. Carla had apparently withdrawn from him, turned critical, and become involved with another man. Now Betty found herself wondering just how much Jon had loved Carla at the beginning. Had she been everything he'd ever wanted? Had they sat together on some honeymoon flight, hand in hand, looking into each other's eyes?

Betty shivered. For some reason, she had never given a thought to Jon and Carla's honeymoon. Suddenly, the thought of it made her extremely uncomfortable. There must have been kisses, embraces, laughter, and warm looks. She shivered again, glancing at Jon and his magazine. Come to think of it, why was he reading a magazine? Why wasn't he talking to her, holding her hand, gazing into *her* eyes?

She decided to walk to the restroom. *Don't create a problem where there isn't one*, she reprimanded herself as she shoved open the lavatory door. *For all you know, they were just as distant as you and Carlton. On the other hand, no one had ever been that distant before!*

Betty made a conscious decision to dismiss Jon and Carla's honeymoon from her mind. It wasn't something she wanted to discuss with him. In fact, it wasn't anything she wanted to know about, now or ever. So she filed it somewhere in her mind's most remote vault, determined to leave it locked away henceforth.

She experienced a twinge of fear as she dismissed Carla and Jon's married life from her consciousness. *Everybody worries about things like that*, she reassured herself. *Besides, I've got him now. And he loves me more than anyone has ever loved me before. That's all I need to know.*

As another day faded into twilight, Hanalei Bay was awash with watercolor hues of violet, indigo, and deep green. Kauai's tropical air was heavy with moisture, and tumbling clouds occasionally splashed massive drops of rain onto the Pacific's tranquil surface. The sea was the temperature of the air, and the air was the temperature of young bodies throbbing with life.

Jon and Betty stood waist deep in the quiet waters, their arms encircling each other, lost in their happiness. Their first days together, with the exception of Betty's wandering worries during the flight to Honolulu, had been wonderful.

This, Betty told herself more than once, *is the real thing! We're really here. It's actually happening. I can't believe it . . .*

It seemed that every time she turned to catch a glimpse of Jon's face, he was already looking at her, a soft expression dancing around his eyes. He was incandescent in his joy, and his smile flooded her with warmth. The delay of the wedding, his interminable captivity, all the doubts, all the lonely days and fearsome nights had been worth the wait. Here was something new to her experience— love that was at the same time peaceful and passionate.

It could be argued that the time the Surrey-Dixons had spent apart had served their relationship well. They had suffered more than ample opportunity to consider each other's character, to weigh the pros and cons of their style of interaction, to assess the future with clear, cold eyes. Their separation had removed them from the hypnotic effect of sensual attraction. Indeed, so removed had they been from the daily habit of one another's company, that at times each of them had considered ending the agony of their love affair's suspended animation.

Could he have put pen to paper, Jon might well have written from his Beirut cell, "Betty, don't wait another day. Get on with your life." He would have gladly let her go, wanting to free her from what he saw as her "obligation" to him, wanting to free himself of his incurable heartache.

And she, in despairing doubt, would have sometimes said, "I can't stand it any more—I can't go on. Please forgive me." More than once she had cried out, "Look, God, just write me out of this never-ending story. If you can't figure out how to finish the book, then find somebody else to star in it!"

Yet, somehow, they had managed to endure, to abide the delay, to hang on to what little hope they'd managed to retain. And now, here they were, bronzing beneath the hot Hawaiian sun, playing in the aquamarine surf, absorbed only in each other and in their gratitude for having "made it through."

Jon was a bright, artistic man. He had a marvelous *joie de vivre* but was not content simply to enjoy the stimulation that normal life offered. He liked to explore and record symbolic moments of people's behavior—international occasions, political upheavals, the impact of one person upon another and of people upon nature. His work took him all over the world, camera in hand, in search of new perspectives on global life. Perhaps because of his personal reserve, he didn't always speak of the things he viscerally understood about people. At times he didn't even speak when he probably should have.

Jon was content to observe without comment. Instead, he often chose to communicate through his photography, speaking with powerful, eloquent images. Jon Surrey-Dixon loved Shakespeare and enjoyed toying with poems of his own in private moments. But socially, as well as professionally, he was a man of fewer words than thoughts.

Betty, on the other hand, was well acquainted with words. With far more than a Sunday crossword puzzler's curiosity, she was deeply devoted to words—both their sight and their sound. She enjoyed placing them in interesting sequences and found several literary outlets for expressing most of her innermost meditations. She had written poetry all her life and was quite capable of labeling the myriad emotions that moved, like kaleidoscopic patterns, through her heart. Because words came so easily to her, she could not comprehend being at a loss for them.

However, in those days, words were not of much concern to either Betty or Jon. They walked, slept, ate, and embraced through carefree days of intense satisfaction. As they learned more about each other, the stunning similarities in their points of view delighted them. They had always enjoyed the fact that they had such complementary opinions. The common ground they shared was a fertile field.

But they also began to find the differences in their approaches to life. Neither of them felt particularly alarmed by these dissimilarities, but they were there nonetheless. Most of these had to do with communication—what seemed proper and necessary and what did not; what should be said and what should remain unspoken. When emotions were at stake, Betty was quick to voice her feelings, unless she feared she would offend. Jon was equally quick to fall silent, unless speaking was unavoidable.

In any case, with only ten days to savor, there was little time for deep deliberation. There were Zodiac boat excursions around the Na Pali coast to be made—wild, water-soaked rides across rollicking seas. There were leisurely drives to tropical glades and helicopter expeditions that lifted them above dizzying pinnacles and plunging chasms. Jon and Betty shared meals of fish and fruits, prepared and served in every conceivable way. Evenings, they dined in fabulous restaurants beneath star-strewn skies, the air fragrant with flowers, the sea whispering in the distance.

In their suite, the two of them adjusted, without a great deal of awkwardness, to the miracle of being together night and day. They laughed as they bumped into each other. They excused themselves politely, attempting to share the clothes closet and the bathroom counter, and the hair dryer.

Tears stung Jon's eyes when, in the middle of the night, he unexpectedly found Betty's hand in his. He was overcome with tenderness and lay awake, humbled with gratitude. He sleeplessly watched the paddles of the ceiling fan send faint breezes into the darkness, stirring Betty's hair and softly moving the bed sheet that covered her bare, suntanned back.

The next morning Betty marveled at the sight of Jon in the kitchen. He was expertly fussing with water and cups and spoons, sending the pungent fragrance of fine Kona coffee into the morning air. When he saw her, he opened his arms without a word, gathering her into his arms and holding her in silent affection.

And so the days passed. The evening before their departure, Jon and Betty walked hand in hand along the water. Barefoot and a little sorrowful that their time in paradise was coming to an end, they had little to say. The water was crystalline as it washed over their feet, and Jon stopped abruptly when he saw a perfect pink seashell lodged in the sand. He quickly scooped it up into his hand, washed it, and handed it to Betty.

"Let's keep it forever. Maybe it will help us remember these wonderful days together."

"How could we ever forget?" Betty whispered, touching the shell with her fingers.

"People forget, Betty. They get busy. They travel. They get distracted. They make mistakes. We have to *choose* to remember. Times like this make all the rest of life worth living."

I'll never forget . . . Betty turned to look back at the footprints in the sand, her blonde hair sweeping across her face, tangled by the afternoon trade winds. *I'll never forget that just once in my life I was really, really happy.*

Jon, who almost seemed to be able to read her mind at times, put his arm around her. "I won't forget either. Because I'm married to the most beautiful, wonderful woman on earth. And don't think I don't know it, Mrs. Surrey-Dixon. You'll never have to remind me of that."

Next morning they were in a far less romantic circumstance. Sweating and frantic to return their rental car, they raced across the tarmac, boarded a rickety Hawaiian Airlines 727, and settled in for the short hop to Honolulu airport. Jon closed his eyes and slept for the duration of the flight.

Betty looked out the window with melancholy eyes, staring into the heart of a massive cloud. Just as they banked for landing, she spotted a rainbow shimmering directly in front of her.

Lord, she silently prayed, *let that rainbow be a sign of Your blessing on our marriage. We love each other so much, I can't imagine anything going wrong. But please—help us with the things we don't know . . .*

Before she could finish her plea, the aircraft touched down. They collected their luggage and made their way to the United terminal.

"I hope your honeymoon was as happy as mine, Betty," Jon hugged her while they waited for their boarding passes. "Did you remember the seashell?"

Betty triumphantly retrieved it from her purse and displayed it in her open palm. "It was definitely the best honeymoon I've ever had!" she laughed. "In fact, I think it's really the only honeymoon I've ever had. Now that I've been with you, Jon, I feel like I've never been married before."

He nodded and smiled and hugged her. But he didn't answer.

Do you feel the same way, Jon? Betty wanted so much to hear him say, "As far as I'm concerned, I've never been married before either, Betty." But he didn't. She couldn't help but wonder why. She couldn't help but ask herself if he'd been equally happy with Carla.

Fortunately, at least for the moment, she kept her questions to herself.

A U-Haul truck idled in front of Betty's Pasadena condominium. It was being driven by Jim Richards, Betty's former boss at Outreach Unlimited Ministries, International and one of Jon's close friends. Jim had agreed to help the newlyweds move to their new apartment in Laguna Beach. Betty had rented her condo to a couple of foreign students from Fuller Seminary. That way, she and Jon could afford a larger home near the ocean.

For several days they had haunted the area that surrounded Victoria Beach, where Betty's childhood dream house stood, flanked by a stone sea tower. Of course the homes along Victoria Drive leased for thousands of dollars a month, if they were available at all. But after an extensive search, Jon and Betty had located a three-bedroom, upstairs apartment on Sunset Drive. It was an older unit with hardwood floors, a fireplace, and a breathtaking view of the ocean.

Once they had secured the residence for themselves, Betty insisted that Jon drive her to the nearest nursery, where she bought a dozen pots of petunias and geraniums. She promptly deposited them in two whitewashed planters outside the living room windows. With the U-Haul on its way from Pasadena, the move was nearly half over. After opening the windows and sweeping the sun deck, Betty had a sudden inspiration. "Jon, we've got to walk down to the beach."

"We don't have time, Betty. The truck is going to be here any minute. Why don't you go by yourself? I'll stay here and wait for Jim. He's not going to be too happy if he gets here and we're at the beach."

"I'll be back by the time Jim arrives."

"You'd better be, or I'll put the furniture in all the wrong places and you'll be mad."

"I don't get mad at you, Jon. I never get mad at you."

"Yes you do. You just don't say so."

There was some truth to Jon's observation. Communicator though she was, Betty was a painfully compliant soul, who hated conflict more than she hated not having things her way. At times she wanted to express minor displeasures or discomforts to Jon. But the issues that troubled her never seemed as important as the serene coexistence they had established in the early days of their marriage. "Peace at any cost" might have been an over-statement of Betty's credo, but she certainly believed in peace at *almost* any cost.

She headed for the staircase that led to Victoria Beach, feeling for the thousandth time that month that things were too good to be true. She almost skipped down the cement steps, hit the sand with both feet, and ran around the rock toward the old stone tower.

The tide was in, and that complicated her mission slightly. She would have to watch the waves care-fully before tearing across the last stretch of beach and scrambling up the rocks at the foot of the tower. Fortunately, years of experience had trained her well. She waited until the undertow carried out the last traces of foam and then dashed to the tower before another set of breakers deluged the sand.

As was her habit, she found a place to sit near the tower and began to watch the water. The diamond on her hand, which now shared her ring finger with Jon's wedding band, flashed in the afternoon light. She began to think back across the years, to her first visit to that rugged, stone-studded beach.

She had been little more than a child—a suffering teenager with excematous skin that ceaselessly itched and peeled. She had come with her stern, religious mother who disapproved of her for almost every reason imaginable. Somehow they had found their way here, of all places, so unlikely a haven for an unaesthetic woman like Lucilla Fuller.

Betty watched the waves crashing against the rocks that guarded the cliffs behind her. She glanced at her hands, at her bare arms that still bore golden traces of the Hawaiian sun. Her skin had not always been so clear and soft. She still remembered how her fledgling faith in God had taken wing one day when she'd thought she'd heard His voice.

"I'm going to heal your skin," the inaudible promise had said.

Her yearning for God's smile bore little resemblance to Lucilla's strict, judgmental doctrines. But in spite of everything else, the two of them claimed the same Christ. And to the amazement of all who heard about it, that first-century Galilean Savior was apparently still in the business of working wonders, no matter what Lucilla said about Him. After more than twenty years of disabling disease, Betty's tortured skin was suddenly well, and just as suddenly Betty was beautiful.

Why did I ever marry Carlton? Betty's love for Jon persistently reminded her that she had settled for far less than "best" the first time around. Although she had gladly received heaven's foretelling of her healing, she hadn't been wise enough to ask for similar information about her first marriage. And her choice to wed Carlton had been about as unheavenly as he was. *I wish I could erase that whole situation from my record.*

There was little comfort in the fact that Jon had made his own mistakes in his first marriage. Betty was so in love with him that she could hardly face the fact that he wasn't perfect. And she fondly wished that he'd been the first man she'd ever lived with. She consoled herself with the vow that he would be the last. No one else would ever own her heart, or, for that matter, touch her body. No one. Ever.

The tide seemed to be rising still, and considering her responsibilities once the truck arrived, Betty reluctantly got up, brushed off her jeans, and stretched. She marched over to the tower and patted it affectionately. "I'll be back tomorrow," she said quietly, glancing around in case anyone appeared unexpectedly. "I live here in Laguna now, you know."

With that, she rushed back up the stairs.

"Perfect timing!" she shouted to Jon as the U-Haul pulled up Sunset Drive.

"It's a good thing you showed up!" Jon yelled back at her. Before long the three of them were hard at work, carrying clothes, furniture, and boxes up the stairs to the new Surrey-Dixon apartment.

Jim suddenly looked up and snapped his fingers. "Oh, Betty, before I forget, there's some mail in the truck for you. It came to OMI and has been piling up since the wedding."

"Thanks, Jim," Betty replied, scurrying down the stairs and climbing into the passenger seat of the truck. She grabbed a handful of letters and sorted through them. Most of them were announcements, notices, and various other bulk-mail items. But one bore what appeared to be a Russian postmark. Another had been mailed from Virginia.

Intrigued by the Russian stamp, Betty ripped open the first letter.

> Dear Elisabeth Casey,
>
> Some friends told us about your work with African children and now we have the book you have written about the Ugandan orphanages. You did a fine job capturing the beauty of those children. We are a Christian couple from British Columbia who are working in Kiev, Ukraine, trying to assist the boys and girls who are suffering the effects of the 1986 Chernobyl nuclear disaster. My husband is a doctor and I am a child psychologist.
>
> We wondered if you and your photographer would consider doing a similar book about our children? We think it would greatly assist the various ministries that support us in our work here. Thank you for considering this idea of ours.
>
> In God's Service,
> Drs. Steven and
> Marion Dunn

Betty smiled and folded the letter back into its envelope. It would take some doing to get OMI or another ministry to finance another children's book. But what a great idea! She couldn't wait to tell Jim and Jon. She started to run inside when she remembered the other letter.

It had no return address. She studied the handwriting for a moment—it looked vaguely familiar. Puzzled, she tore the flap open and pulled out a page of notebook paper, carefully printed in ink.

Dear Betty,

    I got your wedding announcement when I returned from an extended overseas assignment in Eastern Europe. I must admit I read it with mixed feelings. Of course I want you to be happy, and I realize that Jon is a fine man.

    But I want you to know that I find you to be a very unique and beautiful woman, Betty. Something about you has stayed with me, and even though I know as I write this that you are probably already married, you must forgive me for saying that you are unforgettable. And you will always own a part of my heart.

Forever yours,
Mike Brody

Betty was transfixed by the letter. She was alternately horrified, frightened, and deeply touched. Mike Brody was a government agent who was somehow involved in the intelligence community. He had never revealed to Betty who he reported to or what he actually did, but her sense was that he had connections with, in fact probably worked for, the Central Intelligence Agency.

Mike had been of great help and comfort to her during Jon's captivity in Lebanon. He had given her information that she would never have received from the State Department. More than a little good looking, along with his other endearing qualities, Mike had also made some rather romantic moves on Betty in Wiesbaden,

Germany, within hours of Jon's release. Betty had rejected Mike's overtures after a momentary hesitation. Yes, Mike was attractive to Betty. But she loved Jon, and as far as she was concerned, there was no contest between the two.

So what about the letter? She studied it in bewilderment. Of course she couldn't answer; she wouldn't think of answering. But what should she do with it? Burn it? Hide it? File it?

An older, wiser counselor might have suggested that she immediately show the letter to Jon, including him in the predicament. But such a thing never occurred to Betty. For one thing, it might create tension in her happy new home. For another, Jon had been rather distressed with Mike's attention to her in Wiesbaden, and seeing the letter might generate mistrust in his heart. But destroy it? Mike's letter was such a sweet compliment. She couldn't just throw it away, could she?

I'll think about it some other time, Betty concluded. She folded the sheet of paper and stuffed it back into its envelope and then into her jeans pocket. Waving the Kiev invitation, she rushed inside.

"Jim! Jon! Wait till you see this. Somebody wants us to go to Kiev to do another book about children!"

Jim took the letter from her hand and quickly scanned it. He studied Betty's eager face and smiled in spite of himself. "Betty, these things cost money, you know."

"Oh, I know that Jim. But wouldn't it be wonderful if somebody would finance a book like that? I'd love to write it, and Jon would do such a wonderful job on the pictures."

"What pictures? What are you two going on about?"

Jim handed the Dunns' letter to Jon without comment. "I've always wanted to see Kiev," Jon said quietly. "But how excited is anybody going to get about Ukrainian kids and blood disorders?"

"Jon! How can you say that?"

Jon and Jim laughed at Betty's startled expression. "He's talking about marketing, Betty, not humanitarian concerns. Believe me, we'd all be happy to get involved if there were funds available. It's just easier to raise funds for Africa at the moment."

"Why? What's wrong with Ukrainian kids?"

Jon put his arm around her shoulder. "Nothing is wrong with any kids, dear wife. Something, however, is very wrong with the system that we have to use to get things done. It all comes back to the bottom line."

"Well maybe *God* wants us to do this project together," she replied rather sanctimoniously.

Jim looked at the two of them, a fond grin on his face. "That wouldn't surprise me a bit, Betty. And if He does, the money will be there. Why don't you ask Him for it?"

"I will, Jim."

With that, amidst many thanks for his day of toil, Jim headed back to Pasadena with the U-Haul truck, leaving Jon and Betty alone together in their new home. The living room was almost the way they wanted it, thanks to Betty's diligence in putting books in the bookcases while Jim and Jon hauled the heavy boxes to her.

She looked across the room with delight, quite satisfied with the looks of it. "We need a fire in the fireplace, Jon."

"It's not at all cold. We don't need a fire."

"I know it's not cold. But it would be fun anyway, just for atmosphere." With that she ripped up an empty cardboard carton, ignited it with a restaurant match, and sat down on the couch next to Jon. Again she glanced around the room admiringly. He pulled her close to him. All at once she got up and rushed away.

"There's one more thing . . ."

She scurried into the bedroom and located the missing item. Returning to the living room she sat down beside Jon again and placed the pink Hawaiian seashell on the table beside a vase of lavender flowers.

"I told you I'd never forget, Jon."

"I'll never forget, either, Betty. Being married to you is like a dream come true."

As he held her close, Betty heard the crackle of paper in her jeans pocket. Vaguely disgusted with herself, she realized it was Mike Brody's letter. Almost jumping to her feet, she yanked it out of her pocket and threw it into the fireplace. It flared, then crumpled into ashes.

"What on earth was that?" Jon inquired lazily as he stretched out on the couch. He was exhausted.

"Junk mail," Betty smiled sweetly. She picked up the seashell, studied it for a moment, and set it carefully on the table. "Let's go to bed, Jon. You're going to fall asleep on the couch if you don't."

I'll never forget these wonderful days, Jon. She repeated her vow silently as she quickly glanced at the smoldering fireplace and then at the delicate pink shell. *I'll never forget them as long as I live.*

2

A quiet, morning sea washed against the rocks. Betty sat at the base of the Victoria Beach tower, looking south, wondering if the distant airplane high in the sky could possibly be Jon's. She had taken him to Los Angeles International Airport before first light to catch a flight to Central America. His assignment had to do with El Salvador—something for *Newsweek*—and although she wasn't sure about the details, it sounded like he would be relatively safe for the five days he'd be gone. Nevertheless, their separation saddened her a little. Perhaps it brought back memories of his ill-starred departure for Beirut. Or maybe she wanted their first, blissful days of marriage to go on forever. In any case, she was uncharacteristically down in spirit.

At least I've got some things to do to keep me busy, she reminded herself. In spite of the fact that she had mourned Jon's departure for two days prior to their airport farewell, she was pleased to be getting back to work herself. Neither of them had accomplished a thing professionally for almost a month, and although they weren't exactly in financial distress, they soon would be if they didn't get busy. Betty had several freelance writing projects ahead of her, and Jon was beginning a hectic period of international assignments.

While she sat in the morning fog, Betty tried to plan her day. Her first task would be to write a letter to the Dunns. She was fascinated with the possibility of visiting Kiev with Jon. Jim hadn't exactly responded with enthusiasm to the idea, but, on the other hand, he hadn't said, "Forget it!" either. Jim's organization, Outreach Unlimited Ministries, had located financing for Betty and Jon's trip to Uganda and had found a publisher for the book they'd created together about Uganda's children. Perhaps, with some prayer and prodding, Jim might see the possibilities in Kiev—he had a soft spot in his heart for needy boys and girls. In actual fact, so did Betty. But it would be awhile before she fully recognized it.

She had decided to use her morning walk to organize the day, but her mind wandered as usual and she couldn't seem to focus on just what it was she needed to do. She had several magazine articles to write, but none of them were at a drop-dead deadline stage, which meant that she could procrastinate. Nevertheless, she needed to get herself moving in the right direction. She lifted herself off the sandy rock she'd been sitting on and headed up the stairs, along the street, and toward the apartment.

The first time the red Ford Escort drove past her she barely noticed it. The woman at the wheel seemed to be looking for an address, and Betty vaguely observed her gleaming dark brown hair. When the red car slowly cruised by her a second time, however, Betty's curiosity was aroused. Again the Ford slowly made its way along

Victoria Drive, then turned up Sunset, while the driver scrutinized every house along the way.

Just as Betty started toward the apartment, the car came by a third time, and the woman rolled down the window on the passenger side.

"Do you know if Jon Surrey-Dixon lives around here?"

Betty looked into the woman's face. She was extremely pretty, with Italian-looking features and huge brown eyes.

An intuitive alarm went off in Betty's mind, and it jarred her from the inside out. Her palms were instantly damp, and her heart pounded. "Who?" she asked, desperately trying to assess the situation.

"Jon Surrey-Dixon."

Betty frowned, as if searching her mind for a lost piece of information. "Is he married?" she asked the deceitful question as casually as possible, considering the fact that she could barely breathe.

"Yes," the woman laughed inappropriately. "He's a newlywed. I hear that he and his bride"—she hesitated before speaking the word "bride," then nearly spat it out—"moved in somewhere around here."

You're right, Carla. He definitely is a newlywed. So stay away from him, okay?

"If they live around here," Betty answered opaquely, motioning broadly toward several houses at the same time, "They must be out of town."

"I wouldn't doubt it," the woman laughed again. This time Betty noted that there was a strange sound to her laugh—it was forced, a little too loud, and it didn't quite add up with the unmistakable bitterness in her voice. "Jon never stays in one place for more than a week at a time."

The two women's eyes met. *She knows who I am and I know who she is.* A chill grabbed the back of Betty's neck with icy fingers. *The question is, what does she want with Jon?*

"Sorry I can't help you," Betty said quietly, dismissing the intruder by turning away and intentionally heading toward the wrong house.

The woman accelerated abruptly. Her tires smoked as she turned onto the Pacific Coast Highway. Betty waited until the car's red roof disappeared before she found her way up the stairs and in the front door. She was suddenly overwhelmed with dread. Who exactly was that woman? It had to be Carla, but suppose it wasn't? Was there another woman in Jon's life—someone she didn't know about?

Dear God! Was she Lebanese? Maybe while he was a hostage . . . Betty's heart thundered, and then she remembered that the woman didn't have a trace of a foreign accent.

But like a pale, dangerous vapor, mistrust began to blur her scattered thoughts. The woman's words rankled. "Jon never stays in one place more than a week at a time."

It was rather hard to defend Jon on that account because it was essentially true. Surely, in all his adventures, he'd met other women in other towns. So maybe this inquisitive female hadn't been Carla at all. Maybe Jon was a ladies' man—a Lothario—and Ms. Brown Eyes was the mother of his illegitimate child. Or maybe there were several illegitimate children.

After exploring the most inventive and unrealistic mental terrain her brain could possibly envision, Betty finally thudded back into reality. Jon should be given the benefit of the doubt; he was innocent until proven guilty. Unfortunately, Betty complicated that conclusion with a rather unwise determination. *I'm not telling him about this,* Betty vowed. *I don't want him trying to get in touch with Carla or anybody else.*

Betty sank into a melancholy mood after the encounter with the dark-eyed woman. The Surrey-Dixon apartment was lovely, but it was Jon's presence that had breathed life into it. Now it seemed unbearably empty. Betty quickly wiped away unexpected tears and wadded up some newspaper. Stuffing it in the fireplace, she lit a small blaze to counteract the morning's penetrating chill.

Not quite ready to face her computer, she decided to read for a few minutes. Just as she stretched herself out on the floor with a book of psalms and a cup of coffee, the phone rang.

"Betty? Hi, it's Jim. You remember that letter you got from Kiev?"

"Yes, in fact I was just thinking about that Chernobyl children's book idea an hour or two ago."

"Well, maybe God's in it after all. I just heard from a man in Vancouver who apparently knows the people who wrote the letter. His name is Ed Kramer. He's a wealthy guy who finances projects that he feels are worthwhile. Anyway, I guess the Dunns wrote to him and told him about you and Jon. He's interested in talking to you. He's read your book about Uganda, and he was pretty impressed."

"Well, Jon's not here. He left this morning for El Salvador and won't be back till Saturday night."

"That's okay. Kramer didn't seem to be in a big rush. And I don't think he wants to talk to Jon as much as you. He didn't say a word about the photography. Anyway, just give some thought to the possibility of the Chernobyl children's book."

"Jim, I already have. It's never far from my thoughts these days."

"Well, great. You and Jon ought to work together as much as possible. It'll keep you in touch with each other, and besides, each of you brings a lot of talent to your projects. It's interesting, isn't it? Maybe God's going to work this book out after all."

Betty smiled at Jim's parting comment. He was a man of deep faith, if not always tempered with relentless practicality. She suspected that he had done his share of encouraging Kramer. He would have, not only because he cared about the children, but because he knew Jon and Betty were gifted artists who collaborated well on projects like this.

He's one of the good guys. Betty uttered a silent word of thanksgiving for friends like Jim as she opened her book of psalms. Her depression over the pretty stranger had abated, and she deliberately set aside any residual fears as she began to read,

> Make us glad for as many days as you have afflicted us,
>   for as many years as we have seen trouble.
> May your deeds be shown to your servants,
>   your splendor to their children.
> May the favor of the Lord our God rest upon us;
>   establish the work of our hands for us—
>   yes, establish the work of our hands.

The words somehow touched Betty. Was God going to give her gladness for every day she had suffered? She smiled. *That adds up to quite a bit of gladness.*

With Jon's captivity behind them and their marriage happily begun, the Almighty was off to a good start. *Carla or no Carla,* Betty added, inserting a disclaimer as she reviewed the blessings of the past few weeks. Apart from all that, the thing that struck her most forcibly that morning was the thought of God "establishing" the work of her hands.

Betty had begun her writing career as a practical necessity. It was something she did well, and good writing seemed to be a fairly valuable commodity. As time passed, it occurred to her that writing was more than a job—it was a calling. It provided her with a platform from which she could present her ideas and "publish glad tidings," so to speak. Up until now, she hadn't taken her literary skills all that seriously. But something about that psalm, in the wake of Jim's phone call, caused her to stop and think.

"Lord," she said quietly, "I want You to know that my writing belongs to You. If I can help needy children or encourage people or even point them in Your direction with my words, please use me. I know it's all up to You anyway—the work won't come unless You send it. But, just for the record, I'm available. Make me the right person for the projects You have for me, and then send the right projects my way."

Betty's recommitment of her gifts wasn't made casually, but by day's end she had moved it to the back of her mind. All that remained was a renewed sense of purpose and the conviction that she just might have something of value to contribute to the world.

Just at five o'clock, the phone rang. "Hi, Betty. Jim again. Listen, this Kramer guy is really anxious to talk to you—more anxious than I'd realized. Would you be able to fly up to Vancouver early next week?"

"Jon doesn't get home till Saturday, so I can't talk it over with him unless he calls. I doubt that I'll hear from him, but I'm pretty sure he'd agree."

"So shall I tell Kramer you'll be there?"

"Are you going with me?"

"No, it's got nothing to do with me. I'll just set it up—you go by yourself. Kramer's paying for the airfare and hotel, and I'll be sure you're in a nice, safe place. Vancouver's a beautiful city. Have you ever been there?"

"No, Jim. I just wish Jon were going with me."

"Maybe next time. Life's not an endless honeymoon, you know."

Lost in slumber, Betty was jarred awake by the ringing phone. Panic seized her. For a moment she experienced an unpleasant feeling of déjà vu. Jon was still a hostage. She was still waiting to hear that he'd been released. She shook off the false reality and answered.

"Betty? Hi, Sweetheart, it's me. Sorry to wake you."

"Jon, are you all right?" Her voice was shaky.

"Of course I am. Don't worry. My flight's been delayed until very late Sunday night. There's some problem with the airline, a labor dispute or something. I'm really not sure what it is."

Betty tried to summon her drowsy mental faculties. "Sunday night. Okay. Oh, no! Wait a minute. I'm leaving for Vancouver early Monday morning."

"Vancouver? Washington or British Columbia?"

"B.C."

"Why on earth are you going to Vancouver?"

"You remember the Dunns' letter about the children of Chernobyl? Some guy in Vancouver wants to fund the project, and he wants to talk to me about writing the book. You'd be the photographer, of course."

There was a brief pause while Jon processed the news. "That's great, Betty. We'll have to check our schedules to see when both of us can get to Russia."

"As soon as you get back, we can compare calendars. But meanwhile, what time is your flight arriving from down there?"

"About 2:00 A.M.," Jon said.

"I'll see you then," Betty sighed. "I may just stay at the airport and wait for my plane. It takes off at 6:30."

"I'm sorry, Betty, but there's not a thing I can do about it."

"It's not your fault, Jon. I know that. Anyway, I can't wait to see you!"

"How long will you be in Vancouver?"

"Three days."

"Okay. But don't forget, I have to be in New York on Friday."

She had, in fact, forgotten about his New York trip. "Jon, should I cancel my trip to Vancouver?"

He hesitated, "No, I think it's important. Go ahead."

"Jon . . . ?"

"What, Sweetheart?"

"Do you know what kind of car . . ." Her words froze in her mouth. She quickly retrieved herself. "Never mind. It's not worth wasting time long distance. We'll talk about it when you get home."

"Are you sure?"

"I'm sure."

Relieved that she'd stopped short of a discussion of Ford Escorts and those who drive them, nonetheless Betty climbed back into bed with a vaguely uncomfortable feeling. Another dark cloud was trying to form on the horizon of her heart. Jon had been a successful photographer for years, and his eye and expertise were very much in demand. Betty's career was just beginning, but the unexpected success of the Uganda children's book, which featured her text, had brought several new opportunities her way.

Somehow, in her dreams, she had always seen herself as a loving wife, not as a career woman. Yet writing was fulfilling, and she was beginning to see it as something

God could use. The travel it sometimes required was fun, and since Jon was likely to be gone a lot anyway, she might as well stay busy so his absences wouldn't be so painful. Besides, if she worked hard enough and was successful enough, they might be able to work together all the time.

What if the big-eyed brunette shows up while I'm out of town? Betty shuddered. Then, unwilling to succumb to her fears, she reminded herself of Jon and their walk along Kauai's breathtaking beach. Disarmed by a splendid memory, she fell asleep smiling.

She packed her belongings in the car Sunday evening. After reading and rereading the *Times*, watching the news, cleaning the house, and fueling herself with coffee, she headed for the airport at one in the morning. Driving through Laguna Beach in the wee morning hours, she felt a strange hollowness. She and Jon shared life in such a way that a remarkable emotional void occurred inside her when he was absent.

I wonder if he feels that way about me.

As she waited for the stoplight to change, she watched the moonlight dancing on the surf at Main Beach. It was eerily quiet. Not a soul was in sight. Much like her heart, the scene was composed but empty. Without Jon, life seemed devoid of color, of intensity. It looked the same, sounded the same, but his presence made all things vibrant and vivid.

Driving toward the airport, Betty felt frustrated and a little angry. But at whom? It wasn't Jon's fault that his flight was delayed. It wasn't her fault that she'd made arrangements to leave town. Fortunately, it never occurred to her to blame God for the inconvenience His sovereignty sometimes seemed to cause.

She carried her luggage with her and left the locked car for Jon to drive home. Rushing to his gate, she failed to notice the flight-delay notice on the arrival screen. Only after she sank into her seat and stared at the screen for a few moments did the information penetrate her weary brain. The flight definitely would not be arriving at two o'clock. Worse yet, the arrival time was uncertain.

She groaned with fatigue and frustration. Why tonight? Why hadn't she called in advance? Why hadn't she suggested that Jon take a shuttle? Weak with exhaustion and encumbered with what seemed like a ton of baggage, she fought back her tears. What if she didn't get to see Jon at all? How would she get the car keys to him or tell him where it was parked?

The hours dragged on. Betty put her head against her clothes bag and snoozed, woke up, stretched stiffly, and dozed again. *I'm going to be in great shape tomorrow when I meet this Kramer character.*

Finally, at around 4:30, someone posted an ETA for Jon's flight—5:45 A.M. It would be at the gate just forty-five minutes before her flight was to depart, and she had to check in at a different terminal. Anxiety gnawed at her insides. It was impossible to change her plans at this point, otherwise she would have canceled the whole Vancouver fiasco. At the moment, the plight of Chernobyl's children seemed less urgent than her own misery.

Fortunately, Jon's plane arrived ten minutes earlier than predicted. She watched the weary travelers disembark and finally caught sight of her husband's beloved but haggard face. Excitement gripped her. There had never been a time when she hadn't been overjoyed to see him. "Oh, Jon, I was afraid you wouldn't get here before I had to leave!"

He took her in his arms, and they seemed to cling to each other for support. They stood immobile for a few moments, holding one another up. Finally, Jon detached himself from their lengthy embrace, cupped Betty's chin in his hand, and kissed her.

"I sure wish you weren't going to Vancouver."

"Should I cancel?" She searched his face for even the slightest trace of encouragement to do so. *Please say yes!*

"How excited was Jim about this Chernobyl deal?"

"Well, I think he may have put some extra effort into setting it up for us, although he never said so. I just have a hunch he's trying to get us to work on a project together."

"You're probably right. And don't forget, I told him how much I'd like to see Kiev. I guess you'd better go, Betty, although I'm tempted to half-lie and say I'm sick."

She smiled at him fondly. "You don't look sick, Jon."

"I'm just sick of saying good-bye to you."

"Same here . . ."

Jon shoved his luggage into a locker, and they rushed to Betty's departure gate.

"Betty, find out just what this guy wants in terms of pictures and when he wants this thing done. I picked up a couple of new assignments from *Newsweek*, and there's a *National Geographic* piece I might get called for in the Yukon. I've been trying to land that one for a couple of years."

"You do want to work with me on the Chernobyl book, don't you Jon?"

"Of course I do. Why wouldn't I? It's just that these other jobs pay more, and the contacts are really good. We need to work around the other dates if we can, that's all."

By the time they reached the security check at the terminal, Betty's flight was boarding. "Well, that's a record twenty-five minutes together," Jon chuckled. "I'll see you on Wednesday night, right?"

"Right. Eight-thirty, here."

"I love you, Mrs. Jon Surrey-Dixon."

"And I love you, Mr. Jon Surrey-Dixon. I wish I weren't going."

"So do I. Call me when you get to the hotel."

And so she did, and she called him several more times every day. Betty loved to "reach out and touch," as the phone company so warmly put it. She felt each call home was a worthy investment and gladly spent the necessary funds to keep in touch with Jon.

Jon, on the other hand, was less of a phone conversationalist. When he was away, to his way of thinking, he was *away*. He thought about Betty, he missed her, and he even wished she were with him from time to time. But that didn't generate the necessary energy to cause him to call her.

The meetings with Ed Kramer were uneventful, except for the fact that he seemed committed to the Kiev project. He was a short, mustachioed man in his fifties, slightly rotund, with patent leather hair that looked suspiciously like synthetic fibers.

Bald may not be beautiful, but it's got to be better than this. Betty briefly pondered the possible reasons a man of such means would select a bottom-of-the-line toupee. *Just very rich, very eccentric, and utterly devoid of taste,* Betty summed up, wondering why his wife didn't insist that he have a hair transplant.

"I've known the Dunns for years," he explained over lunch at the Holiday Inn. "They are the most wonderful people you could ever know. He's a quiet country doctor, and she's a woman who understands people from the inside out. I don't think she learned a thing from her education in psychology. She could have hung out her shingle without ever going to college."

"What does she do in Kiev?"

"Oh, they're working together on all kinds of studies about the children's health, attitudes, feelings about life and death, and on the changes in parent-child relationships that happen in the face of serious illness. The Dunns have done some landmark studies. I hope you can feature them a little bit in your book."

What I hear you saying, Mr. Kramer, is that I WILL feature them in my book. "Of course," Betty smiled kindly. "I understand, because my husband and I enjoy working together, too. He was the photographer on the Uganda book, you know."

Kramer nodded absently. "I've got a son-in-law who's a photographer . . ."

Betty hesitated, not sure it was the right occasion to probe about schedules and details. Enough of Kramer, anyway. She'd met him, and he seemed satisfied with her. Why did she need to stay in Vancouver three days? What else did they need to talk about?

Ed Kramer dismissed her from the day's explanations and exhortations before sunset, and Betty found herself walking around the streets of the immaculate Canadian city, looking in shop windows, admiring myriad flower beds that seemed to outnumber the pedestrians, and checking her watch. That night, feeling quite satisfied that she'd gleaned enough expectations from Ed Kramer's rather unimaginative brain, she called Jim Richards.

"Jim, I'm not feeling my best," she fibbed, trying to rationalize by focusing her mind on a mild case of indigestion. "What would happen if I tried to get home tomorrow morning instead of tomorrow night?"

"Did you tell Ed?"

"No, I didn't get a chance."

"Well, call him at home and see what he says. Are you all right?"

"Oh, yeah, I'm really fine. Just my stomach."

"And your heart, I suspect." Jim knew Betty better than she thought he did.

"My heart?"

"Don't tell me you don't miss that photographer of yours. And even if you don't, he misses you. I talked to him tonight. Go ahead and try to get home early. I'll deal with Kramer if he doesn't like it."

The next evening found Betty poring over several books and periodicals about the Chernobyl disaster. Jon walked in with two bags of groceries.

"Taking a crash course in nuclear reactor meltdowns?" he commented, glancing at her as he made his way into the kitchen.

"This is just background stuff, Jon, so I don't make a fool of myself."

"Don't you have some writing to do for that music magazine? How would you like for me to make dinner tonight?"

"I've got an article half-done in there, and I should Fed Ex it tomorrow. I'd love for you to make dinner, if you don't mind." Jon liked to experiment in the kitchen, and now and then he created something quite spectacular.

He sat down beside her on the floor and took her in his arms. "I have some plans for you later on this evening that don't include your computer or this pile of papers," he motioned to the books spread around them. "I was thinking in terms of something a little more stimulating than environmental crisis management."

Dinner was served, an hour or two of work was completed, and Jon and Betty retired to their bedroom, sharing the deep intimacy they'd somehow won for themselves in the midst of life's battles. Just as they were about to fall asleep, the phone rang.

Betty answered. A woman's voice, slightly muffled and sounding rather tentative, said, "Is this the residence of Jon Surrey-Dixon?" For some reason, Betty immediately thought of the woman in the red car.

"Yes it is. Just a moment."

She handed the receiver to Jon with a shrug.

"Hello?" he said, "Yes? Oh, hi."

Something in his tone made Betty uncomfortable. Who was the woman? She started to leave the room, but curiosity restrained her.

"Yeah," Jon was speaking in monosyllables. "That was my wife . . . No, I don't think so . . . Why? . . . I see . . . How long have you been there? . . . I'm not sure that's such a good idea right at the moment . . . Uh, yeah . . . Well, I'll think about it."

He hung up with a look on his face that Betty had never seen before. It was puzzled. It was troubled. It was confused and perhaps a little embarrassed.

For some reason she was almost afraid to speak. "Who was that?" she said, her back to him, trying to look interested in a book she'd taken off a shelf.

There was a pause. "It was Carla."

Betty felt a surge of fear and pain. "Carla? What does she want?"

Jon was silent, lost in his own thoughts. "Jon, what is it?" Betty's voice was almost hoarse. She felt extraordinarily threatened.

"Betty, it's nothing to do with us. She's in a . . . well, she's involved in some kind of therapy. And the psychiatrist she's working with wants her to talk to me about what went wrong with our marriage. It's part of her, uh, treatment. I'm not sure what she's talking about, and I'm not sure I want any part of it."

"Jon, that's ridiculous! Why should she dig up the past now? Doesn't she know you're married?"

"She asked me who answered the phone, and I told her."

"How did she get our number?"

"Through a man I work with now and then. She still talks to his wife occasionally."

Betty went into the bathroom and shut the door. She stared into the mirror, trying to understand the uncomfortable apprehension that was mounting inside her. Was she having a premonition of trouble ahead? Was she just reacting to the intrusion of another woman? Why did Carla's former place in Jon's life make her feel so vulnerable?"

She's so pretty . . . God help me. She turned on the water so Jon would think she was washing her face or teeth or something. She continued to stare into the mirror. The face that stared back at her was white, wide-eyed, and afraid. The blonde hair was disheveled because Jon had been running his fingers through it. Their times together were always tender, and tonight had been no exception—until now.

Jon was leaving tomorrow for New York, and that made Betty all the more restive. She had a thousand questions racing around in her mind, but she was afraid to ask them. As much as she wanted to know the truth, she couldn't face the pain it might inflict on her. She turned off the water and flushed the toilet, still staring.

How much had he loved Carla? How hard did he try to make it work with her? How good were their good times? How badly did they treat each other? What did he do wrong to contribute to their divorce?

She returned to the bedroom, trying to look nonchalant. Jon was in bed, on his side, his back to her. She stretched herself out between the sheets and tried to relax. Was he asleep? Or was he shutting her out?

"Jon?" she whispered.

"Hmmm?"

"Are you awake?"

"Sort of . . ."

"Jon, what about this Carla thing? What are you going to do?"

"I don't know yet, Betty. I need to think about it. Don't worry, Sweetheart. It's got nothing to do with you. Go to sleep." He rolled over and gave her a hug, then returned to his semi-fetal position.

Betty lay awake for two hours listening to Jon's even snoring, fighting her fears, and trying to sort out her impressions. Suddenly, impulsively, she got up out of bed, pulled on some sweats and shoes, and slipped out the front door.

You're crazy to go out in the middle of the night—the first person you see will be a serial killer. Or, worse yet, a Sophia Loren-type in a red Ford.

Nevertheless, Betty's restlessness prevailed. She scurried down the steps to the beach, and began to walk. She didn't go toward the tower but headed off in the other direction, taking long, deliberate strides. Occasionally she glanced at the darkened beach houses that cast odd, oblong shadows across the sand. There wasn't another person in sight.

Walking and thinking, she gradually felt her fear dissipate and weariness begin to take its place. Was she overreacting to the phone call? Probably. She was an emotional woman and fear of abandonment was no stranger to her. She turned and headed home.

Her thoughts began to focus on a few lines of verse that suddenly entered her head. Maybe they were a reflection of her insecurities. Maybe they were a prayer. She wrote them out on the back of an envelope before she fell asleep beside Jon, who never knew she'd left. Once the words were poured out across the paper, Betty released Carla's call from her mind—at least for the moment.

> Back to the sea I've found my way
> To glistening waves and misting spray,
> Ceaseless the tides where dolphins play—
> Never-changing sea.
> Wild blow the storms, and breakers roll,
> Followed by calm, when white gulls soar;
> Raging or restful, sea meets shore—
> It must ever be.
> Oh, God, but footprints wash away,
> And, like the pale mist, love won't stay,
> Grant from Your sea one gift I pray—
> Teach me constancy.

Jon seemed quite himself the next morning. He didn't mention the call, but he was warm and affectionate. Of course he had to leave for the airport, and therefore another separation was about to begin. Would it always be this way? Betty mulled the thought over in her mind as she drove home alone from the airport—again. Now she was beginning to travel, too. Would that relieve the problem, or double it?

Most married couples go to work every day at businesses some distance from their homes. They don't see each other from eight o'clock till dinner time, and when they do they may well be too tired to talk. At least when she and Jon were both in town, they had some quality time to enjoy each other. Still, she wished they could be together far more and that he would phone more frequently when they were apart.

I wonder if he'll call Carla from New York. Suddenly a cold dread gripped her. Maybe he'd been talking to Carla all along, and she just hadn't known about it. *That's absurd. He loves me! He treats me like a queen. Why am I putting myself through this?*

Once she got home, she began in earnest to complete the article for the *Ministry Musician* magazine. It was a feature about the history of music in the church and the evolution of hymns into songs of praise and worship. She pulled an old hymnal off the shelf and started to type the beloved words of "Just As I Am." One of the verses caught her eye.

> Just as I am,
> Though tossed about
> With many a conflict
> Many a doubt,
> Fightings within and fears without,
> Oh, Lamb of God, I come, I come.

Tears flooded her eyes. *That's me.* She shook her head in resignation. *Even when there's nothing wrong on the outside, I'm still fighting fear on the inside.*

"Oh, God, please take away my fears and doubts. After everything You've done for me, they just shouldn't be there . . ."

The phone rang. She picked it up and said, "Hello," but no one responded. After a couple of seconds the other party hung up.

Carla. It was her. I know it.

That dread again—it came rushing back like a bitter tide, intent on drowning her peace of mind. Her hands shook a little as she returned to her computer and tried to get her mind back on what she was doing. After five minutes, the phone rang again.

"Hello?" she answered sharply.

"Hello, Betty? It's your old man."

Harold Fuller, Betty's father, was a salty ex-Marine. She was always happy to hear from him, although their relationship hadn't always been as cordial as it was now. Before Betty's mother died, Harold had found little time for his only daughter—devotion to his wife had precluded any other emotional ties.

But since his wife's passing, and in part because he had chosen to involve himself with Betty during Jon's captivity, Harold was more interested, more caring, and more of a real father to her.

"Oh, Daddy! Hi!" She hadn't talked to him since she'd returned from her honeymoon. "Did you try to call me a few minutes ago?"

"No, I just walked in the door. I've been meaning to call for a week but just haven't picked up the phone."

"What have you been doing?"

"Oh, you know. Keeping the refrigerator empty and the woodshed full is enough to wear me out."

Harold's Oregon mobile home was kept at a constant eighty-five degrees, and his waistline seemed to be nearly that many inches. Betty laughed outloud. "At least you aren't bored."

"Nope, I'm never bored. What's new with you?"

Betty told him briefly about the possible Kiev trip and touched on the various other projects she was doing. She avoided mentioning Carla.

"Is that man of yours treating you right?"

"Daddy, he's wonderful. He treats me the way every woman wants to be treated. I just hope it stays that way."

"Well, don't start borrowing trouble. Why wouldn't it stay that way?"

"Honeymoons don't last forever, you know. In fact he's gone now, to New York. He'll be back Sunday."

"I don't like all this traveling he does. Your mother and I . . ."

"Daddy, now who's borrowing trouble? I knew he traveled when I married him. He has to travel. And I'm starting to do a little traveling, too," she added proudly.

Harold wasn't impressed. "You stay home and take care of your house. There's nothing wrong with doing a writing job or two, that's fine. But keep a clean house and cook good meals. That way he'll always want to come home."

"Well, I hope he can find a better reason to come home than that!"

"Yeah, well that, too."

Betty and her father concluded their conversation on a congenial note. Hearing the sound of his voice was comforting to her somehow, and she was grateful for the rapport they'd finally developed. Eventually she was engrossed in her work and her spirits began to rise. By the time she finished and started to fix herself something to eat, Carla seemed less significant than before.

Just before she went to bed, the phone rang again. The caller paused and hung up after Betty said hello. *It's her. I know it's her.* Betty was annoyed and frustrated. What if Jon had been there? Would he have had another cryptic chat with his ex-wife? Why hadn't he simply told her not to call again and let it go at that?

By 9:45, Betty was incoherent—her wee-hours expedition the night before caught up with her, and she decided that a good night's repose was in order. Fearing another interruption by the mystery caller, she took the phone off the hook, pulled the pillow over her head, and drifted into a deep sleep.

Three thousand miles away, Jon dialed and redialed their number. Who was she talking to? Maybe the phone was out of order. He was excited about a new job he'd landed and wanted to tell her about it.

I wonder if Carla called back, he pondered that unpleasant possibility before turning the light out. *She's such a troublemaker. Maybe I should have told Betty she's been admitted into a hospital. But what if she starts threatening Betty, too? She'll do anything she can to cause trouble—I just hope that's not why the phone's busy. But who else would Betty be talking to? And why?*

It was well past 1:30 A.M. Eastern Time when Jon finally went to sleep himself. Carla's calls worried him. He wanted to focus all his attention on Betty, and the thought of going back over old, chronic problems was extremely distasteful to him. Carla was forever angry, and no matter what he said or did, she'd end up hating him for it.

Dragging Betty through all that was unthinkable. *The less said, the better,* he concluded. *If I don't bring it up, Betty won't either. The last thing she needs to know is how crazy Carla really is.*

3

_____

The sleek jetliner pierced the Canadian sky, engines shrieking, as it made its final approach to Vancouver Airport. Sensing her apprehension, Jon took Betty's hand, as he always did on takeoffs and landings when they flew together. A seasoned traveler, he had long ago overcome any fear of flight he might have had in his youth. As for Betty, although she tried to hide her disquietude, it was evident in her stiffened posture, rapid breathing, and furtive glances out the window. He could almost hear her thoughts: *Will the flaps work? Will the tires blow out? Will the pilot hit a slippery spot on the runway and lose control?*

Betty smiled at Jon, and he shook his head in amusement. "You're such a neurotic!" he laughed.

"Not when you're around," she smiled back at him. "You've almost cured me, you know."

Ed Kramer had called Betty back to Vancouver for another meeting about the Kiev book. "Should Jon come with me this time?" she had asked, praying for a yes. She got one, and the arrangements were made. This time

Vancouver was an adventure, not an intrusion on her honeymoon. When she and Jon weren't sitting in Kramer's posh Hastings Avenue office, they were exploring historic Gastown, riding the Seabus to the North Shore, or browsing around Chinatown.

Betty was buoyant, striding along beside her husband. "It doesn't seem like the same city with you along, Jon. It's really beautiful!"

"I don't think you gave it a fair chance the last time, Betty. You were tired and didn't want to be here."

"That's not what I mean. I mean when you're around, everything is more fun, more wonderful . . . I don't know. It's just different."

Jon didn't reply, but he smiled and hugged her. His face revealed only pleasure.

No matter how happy she was, however, Betty was greedy for reassurances. *I wish he'd say, "That's just the way I feel . . ."* Having allowed the thought to surface, Betty quickly upbraided herself for wanting more attention than she was getting. *You're never satisfied!*

Besides, maybe men just weren't the greatest communicators. Some women seem to think that males aren't only the world's worst communicators, but they have nothing worthwhile to say even when they try. Betty didn't feel that way. She liked men, in fact some of the men she'd known had been downright lovable.

Unfortunately, Ed Kramer didn't fit into the "lovable" category, at least not in Betty's small but well-detailed book. In fact, this time around, she could hardly bear him. The Surrey-Dixons' meetings with him were disconcerting, at least to her. In his mild, eccentric way, he was clearly accustomed to having things according to his schedule and by his set of specifications. But far worse, and to Betty's growing consternation, he completely ignored Jon in every conversation. In fact he never addressed him at all, except to say, "Hello, how are you, nice to see you," or "Good-bye, thanks for coming, see you later."

Relaxed but silent, Jon sat at Betty's side while she and Ed discussed the various possibilities of the Kiev book. Betty had developed a rough outline, and Ed appeared to be fairly satisfied with it. He wanted to feature the Dunns, of course. He was also quite interested in the various Ukrainian children's hospital facilities, in showing the ailing children at home with their parents, and in presenting a brief history of Kiev as a cradle of Christianity.

That last subject seemed out of place in the book Betty was developing in her mind. Why get into early Eastern Orthodox history? It was incongruous with everything else that needed to be said. She kept her own counsel for the time being. There was another matter that troubled her far more.

When Betty tried to include Jon in the conversations, Kramer nodded politely but refused to acknowledge him. In fact, with every passing hour, he seemed more intent on excluding Jon completely.

"Jon, how do *you* feel about the Kiev monasteries?" Betty inquired, rather impatiently, at one point in the conversation. She reached over and touched his hand, desperately wanting to draw him into the discussion whether Kramer wanted him to participate or not.

"I think they photograph beautifully. I have some shots of some similar Eastern European churches in my portfolio, and they're quite dramatic."

Again Kramer nodded but didn't respond by asking to see the photographs.

Finally the worst happened. During the last meeting on the last day, as if Jon were totally invisible, Ed remarked, "My son-in-law has taken some great pictures of Kiev, and he's known the Dunns for years. I'd like to send him over there to do the shooting for this book of ours. He's got a new Minolta rig that does everything for him but develop the pictures. I gave it to him for his birthday," he added proudly.

Betty was mortified. Hadn't Kramer understood that she and Jon were working as a team? Should she speak up now, or wait until Jon was out of the room? She felt oddly protective of her husband, convinced that he had been gravely wounded by Kramer's insensitivity. How could she quickly and completely rectify the situation?

She peeked at Jon, who looked surprisingly at ease. What was wrong with him? Didn't he understand that they weren't going to Kiev together after all? Glancing at the clock on Kramer's desk, Betty stood up. She spoke more assertively than was her habit. "Mr. Kramer, it's nearly five, and I have to make a phone call. If you feel we've covered everything enough, maybe we'll just excuse ourselves now."

Kramer seemed rather surprised at the abrupt conclusion to his meeting. Nevertheless, he was a professional man and a busy one. Surely he had spent ample time with this young couple. His fortune was in silver mining, not in Christian books about needy children. If he could do the Dunns a favor while giving his son-in-law an opportunity to get some professional photography experience under his belt, he would be quite satisfied.

Betty was fuming by the time the elevator settled onto the ground floor. "How could he do that? How could anybody be so rude? He acted like you were invisible!"

Jon laughed at her outburst. "Betty, he wants you for the job, not me."

She stared at him in disbelief. *How can you be so detached?* "Look, Jon, the only reason I took this job was so we could work together. I don't want to go all the way to Kiev alone. Besides, why did he fly you up here if he wants me and not you? What a jerk!"

"Hey, he's probably into family values. You told him we were newlyweds, didn't you? Maybe he thinks it's his Christian duty to include your husband in your business deals. Anyway, Betty, it's not a problem, believe me. We got a free trip to Canada, all expenses paid. Besides, I've got more work coming up than I can handle. By the way, there's no reason for you to back out of this opportunity just because he wants his son-in-law to take the shots."

"Jon, the only reason the Uganda book did well was because of your world-class photographs. Anybody could have written the text. The pictures said it all."

"Well, Kramer obviously doesn't see it that way." Jon's voice was beginning to sound a little edgy. "Enough. Let's go to dinner."

He's got to be upset. Everybody knows that male egos can't handle this kind of thing. He's humiliated, but he's too proud to admit it, and he doesn't want to upset me.

Betty's thoughts tumbled over each other in a rather disorderly fashion. She took into consideration feminism's view of female power. How would *New Woman* magazine address her plight? What about *The Total Woman* or its flip side, *Women Who Love Too Much?* Was she feeling codependent, independent, or interdependent? She contemplated her priceless, newly born marriage and God's promise to establish the works of her hands. All these passed through her consciousness in just a few seconds.

What was she supposed to do? Be a powerful woman, an individuated woman, a "total" woman, a submissive woman, a troubled woman, or a sacrificial woman who would give up anything for her man?

What were the rules of the game anyway? If she and Jon tried to talk about Kramer's dismissal of Jon, he would adamantly deny being upset. She, in turn, would find that unbelievable and would silently accuse him of being dishonest. But, above all else, she'd be too afraid of an argument to confront him. On the other hand, if they ignored the whole thing, it could emerge, Phoenix-like, months later, in some fiercer, more malevolent form.

If you err, err on the side of reticence, someone had once instructed her. She remembered the saying but forgot that the person who'd said it had been both calculating and emotionally detached. And so it was, without another word, that the Surrey-Dixons went to dinner. They flew home the next morning.

Back in Laguna Beach, while Betty was putting away her clothes, Jon was checking the answering machine. "Any messages?" she called out from the next room.

"Nothing much . . . ," he said quietly.

"Who called?"

"Oh, Jim wanted to know about the trip. You'd better fill him in about Kramer's son-in-law. And Carla called again."

"Jon, what does she want? Is she trying to get you back?"

Jon sighed heavily. Why had he even mentioned the call? Now Betty would be upset for the rest of the day. "No, and even if she was, it wouldn't matter. I love *you*, Betty. That's all there is to it."

A couple of hours later, Jon kissed her good-bye. He had to go to Ventura for the night to meet with some environmentalists involved in the Yukon story. He was unusually excited about that particular assignment, and

Betty was glad to see that he would soon be sitting down and having serious planning meetings. Maybe it wasn't all talk after all.

She decided to hash things over with Jim Richards while Jon was gone. When she poured out the story of Kramer's rudeness toward Jon, Jim seemed surprisingly unconcerned. "Oh, Kramer's an oddball. Don't worry about it. Jon doesn't need that kind of headache any-way—he's got plenty of work. By the way, I've got another job for you here."

"What kind of a job?"

"Oh, there's a guy in Florida with a little ministry to the street people. He wants to write a book about the homeless in Fort Lauderdale.

Perfect. While you're at it, why don't you find something for me to write about Christian mortuaries? Or how about an international assignment—maybe some success stories from a twelve-step recovery clinic in Iraq?

"Thanks, Jim," she responded as enthusiastically as possible, jotting down the number with a pen that didn't work. I'll give him a call." *Sometime in the year 2050.*

As far as making career plans was concerned, Betty didn't have a clue. She was only capable of reacting, not of taking any kind of action herself. Whatever jobs came her way, if she could stomach them, she took them. Whenever jobs didn't work out, she said, "Good riddance; who needs it?" Her only concern was with the possible spiritual impact her words might make on readers and, of course, the ensuing paycheck.

Her personal goals revolved around Jon, their mar-riage, and their future together. She had taken to heart the concept that "Love covers a multitude of sin," and it was her heartfelt hope that love would somehow erase her first marriage from existence, along with the sense of failure her divorce had imparted.

She found it impossible to view her years with Carlton Casey as a learning experience or a growth opportunity. Carlton's unfriendly manner and unimpassioned personality had never been easy to bear. But when she thought about it, her greatest struggle was with the awful truth that she had come all too close to being unfaithful to him. A powerful physical encounter with an old friend, Jerry Baldwin, had nearly swept away every vestige of her morality, propriety, and good sense. Not long after that near miss, Betty had left Carlton—primarily because she knew she could never be faithful to him.

Then there had been Mike Brody. Through the worst of times, Betty had waited for Jon's release from captivity believing with all her heart that they were meant to be together. Yet on Jon's very first night of freedom, Mike had reached out to her and she had responded, at least at first. After a few reckless moments, she had pulled herself away from him and rushed back to Jon. But the guilt of having been enamored, however briefly, had never quite left her.

Betty, you're such a femme fatale. She shook her head, sighed, and glanced heavenward. *Completely irresistible.*

In both cases, she had been seeking emotional support wherever she could find it. Innately she knew she had a craving for more affection and attention than anyone could possibly give to her. Because of Jerry and Mike, she mistrusted herself implicitly. True, she'd never actually committed adultery with either of them, but she'd given herself a couple of good scares and dished out a somewhat humiliating disappointment to each of them.

But that was before her marriage to Jon. Now, if she could just make their relationship perfect by doing everything right, by making no mistakes, by making no waves and causing no problems, nothing would ever go wrong again. Jon was everything she'd ever wanted, and their marriage *had to work.* There were no alternatives. If it didn't, she would never again be able to live with herself.

All this was going on in her mind as she sat in front of the living-room fireplace. Beyond her, a dramatic sweep of Pacific Ocean glistened green beneath a pale sky. In that moment, sitting motionless, with a coffee mug between her hands and a shaft of afternoon light illuminating her golden hair, Elisabeth Surrey-Dixon was extremely beautiful.

No one but God Himself had the opportunity to admire her; no one else was there to appreciate the striking study in composition and color. And Betty, least of all, could have never seen herself as fondly as He did, so pensive in the late-day quietness. She could not have imagined His viewing her without a thought of condemnation. She had never conceived of the fact that He was quite delighted with her just the way she was.

The vision passed with the ringing of the phone. This time the muffled woman's voice was less timid. "Is Jon Surrey-Dixon there?"

"May I ask who's calling?" *As if I didn't know.*

"This is Carla Samuels."

Betty was determined to keep her tone even—to maintain control. After all, she was his wife. "Jon isn't here, Carla. He won't be back for several days." By now Betty was almost completely convinced that Carla had been the driver of the red car. *I wonder if she recognizes my voice.*

"So he's still a traveling man, is he?" The woman laughed too loudly. "Some things never change."

"Shall I take your number?" *Of course I'll never give it to him, but I might as well pretend I'm going to.*

"He already has it. Besides, you wouldn't give it to him anyway."

Touché. Betty was stunned by Carla's stinging, albeit accurate response. "I'll tell him you called, Carla." She hung up without allowing herself to say another word.

She immediately dialed Jon's hotel. To her surprise he answered. "Jon, did I wake you up?"

He fibbed, his voice thick with sleep. "No, no I was just lying down. We're taking a break between meetings."

"Carla just called again. And she wasn't particularly nice to me."

"No, I don't suppose she was."

"Jon, does she want you back? Why is she calling all the time? Why would she be rude to me?"

He laughed in spite of himself. "Why *would* she be rude? Why *wouldn't* she be rude? Are you kidding? She's rude to everybody. She's a very unhappy lady, Betty. Pity her and don't worry about it."

Feeling faintly reassured, Betty went to her computer and began to work. She found herself making excellent progress. In fact she finished two jobs before she went to bed that night.

As was sometimes her custom, she decided to read a few verses before she went to sleep. She pulled her Bible into her lap, propped herself up with pillows, and thumbed through the gilt-edged pages.

> Let love and faithfulness never leave you;
>   bind them around your neck,
>   write them on the tablet of your heart.
> Then you will win favor and a good name
>   in the sight of God and man.
> Trust in the LORD with all your heart
>   and lean not on your own understanding;
> in all your ways acknowledge him,
>   and he will make your paths straight.

She looked up from the page. For some reason the words brought a flutter of hope to her heart. She thought about the problem with Kramer. The beautiful woman in the red Ford. The calls from Carla. Her obsessive desire to have a perfect marriage.

"Let love and faithfulness never leave you . . ."

She had loved, but she had not always had a faithful heart. That was a well-worn entry in her catalog of failures. As for "leaning on her own understanding," she was a master at trying to figure things out, trying to analyze, ad nauseum, every aspect of every circumstance. She mulled things over until they physically made her head ache. Maybe this was a message to her about that, too.

In any case, before she could receive any further spiritual benefit from the passage, the phone rang. Her anxiety rippled through her. "Hello?"

Silence. Click.

She slammed the receiver down. *That . . .* One particularly impolite word came to mind. She dismissed it and tried to settle down.

Trust in the Lord with all your heart . . .

The words suddenly reappeared in her mind. She tried to apply them to her circumstances. Did she trust in the Lord with all her heart? Not even half, she suspected. She was too busy trying to figure things out, trying to make things work, trying to do things right. Besides, what was she supposed to trust Him with, and what was she supposed to do herself? She'd never quite gotten that part straight.

She rolled over and the phone rang again. Furious, she nearly tore the receiver loose from the cord. "Yes?" she barked.

"Betty?" Jon sounded rather taken aback.

"Oh, Jon! I'm sorry. I thought you were . . ."

"Did she call back?"

"Someone did. Whoever it was hung up when I said hello."

"It must have been her, Betty. Please don't worry, okay? I'm going to go over and see her on my way back—she's out in the San Fernando Valley now. I want to get this settled once and for all."

"You're going to see her? Why? What makes you think that'll keep her from calling?"

There was a long pause—too long for Betty's liking. Jon finally replied, "Betty, you're going to have to trust me on this one."

They said good-bye, and he told her to unplug the phone, which she did. But sleep eluded her, at least for a few hours. *Trust in the Lord with all your heart . . .* That phrase was spinning around her head like a gyroscope, interrupted only by . . . *and lean not on your own understanding.*

If anyone had been there to ask, Betty would have answered quite honestly that she wasn't trusting the Lord at all. Probably for that very reason, she was performing an astonishing array of cognitive calisthenics. She wanted to understand every action, every conversation, every situation, and every motive of everybody she knew— most notably Jon Surrey-Dixon and his ex-wife. And she was futilely trying to gain that understanding, even though it was not meant for her to know.

It would have been an ideal opportunity for someone to advise, "Look, Betty, why don't you just lighten up and enjoy being happily married to a man who adores you?" But even the Wonderful Counselor's attempts to encourage her along those lines had fallen on deaf ears. Betty was determined to make her second marriage flaw- less, to search out any and every threat, and to go to war against it. Her efforts amounted to an exceedingly tiresome business. It wasn't peace that finally lulled her to sleep. It was sheer mental exhaustion.

In the months that followed a faint chill crept into the Surrey-Dixon apartment. It wasn't the sea wind, although late in the afternoon the Pacific breeze could be bracing. It wasn't the frost of changing seasons, despite the fact that autumn, winter, and summer had passed with little variation. An almost imperceptible coolness grew between Betty and Jon. It didn't affect their lovemaking or their laughter or their appetites. It didn't cause them to avoid each other or to consciously think ill of one another. It was a subtle, almost intangible change.

Jon had seen Carla and her psychiatrist on several occasions since the phone calls began. He had told Betty when he was going and when he would be back. There was no secrecy to the visits, at least with regards to their time, place, and purpose. "She and her therapist are trying to determine what kind of behavior patterns have caused her to have so many problems. She's very depressed, Betty. And she's divorced again."

Naturally, that little nugget of information did nothing for Betty's confidence or attitude. She was all the more suspicious of Carla's motives, imagining her lonely and predatory, reaching back to the sweet tender love she and Jon had most certainly shared. Betty was also displeased with the fact that Jon wouldn't discuss his meetings with Carla and the counselor. He refused to talk to her about them, just shaking his head and saying, "Betty, it's not important. I love you. That's all that matters."

It isn't all that matters. I need to know every detail of every conversation. You're hiding something. I know you are, Jon! Don't play games with me.

She replayed those same thoughts a thousand times, but she could never quite bring herself to speak them aloud. She didn't want to deal with the possibilities. So, quite unconsciously, she settled instead for a low-level cold war. Even to herself she barely acknowledged the shadowy resentment that had settled over her world. It felt more like sadness than anger, and so she catered to it like a melancholy mood. She withdrew. She read. She wrote. She became increasingly self-centered. All the while, she treated Jon with impeccable courtesy.

Jon, in the meantime, had become exceedingly busy. He was traveling at least two weeks out of every four. When he was home, Betty's quiet, polite distance puzzled him. He felt he had protected her from any hurtful information regarding his first marriage. He had chosen to be meticulously close-mouthed about Carla's outbursts, accusations, and criticisms—and hospitalization.

Of course, part of his silence came from the humiliation he felt in the face of Carla's attacks. Even her therapist was stunned by her vitriolic assaults. But Jon felt he was doing the right thing by going to the sessions. He hadn't made much effort to discuss her problems before, so relieved had he been by her departure. He hadn't seen much point in trying to improve his marriage to Carla. He had simply divorced her when she got involved with husband number two, a stranger to him who was now ex-husband number two. Now he was willing to learn anything that might help him be a better husband to Betty.

Jon still held Betty tightly in his arms from time to time, and she continued to respond to his embraces with passion and warmth. Their times of intimacy made him feel that things weren't so bad. And Betty, who craved his affection more than ever, wasn't about to withdraw from their physical relationship. At least she found herself close to him then. In the quiet tenderness of their bedroom, nothing seemed to be wrong.

Throughout the year, Betty's Kiev project continued to simmer on Ed Kramer's back burner. He was waiting for some check or other income to come in—then the trip would be scheduled. And Jon's Yukon expedition was set to depart in late May—in time for the spring thaw. He was looking forward to it with growing excitement. Communications would be difficult, and he would certainly miss Betty. But it was the dream of a lifetime for him. He couldn't wait.

Meanwhile, the calls from Carla persisted. They were almost always in the evening, lasting only one or two minutes, and Jon always spoke in monosyllables. But still they came a couple of times a week. Sometimes Betty glanced out the window, expecting to see the red Ford. It never came.

One evening, Jim drove from Pasadena to Jon and Betty's apartment. They had invited him and his assistant, Joyce Jiminez, to dinner. Joyce was a dear friend of Betty's, and she couldn't wait to see her.

Getting Joyce's wheelchair—and Joyce—up the stairs to the apartment was a major production. Her very life appeared to be in grave jeopardy at least a dozen times as Jon and Jim awkwardly hoisted their precious cargo upward, one step after another. Joyce couldn't walk, but she could laugh. And laugh she did.

After dinner, Jim and Jon went for a walk on the beach. After Betty finished cleaning up the kitchen, she and Joyce sat down in the living room together. Joyce had been with Betty in the early days of her romance with Jon, had staunchly supported her through his Beirut captivity, and had been the matron of honor at their wedding. Although they had spoken on the phone a few times since Jon and

Betty moved to Laguna Beach, this was their first chance to really visit.

"So how does it feel to be Mrs. Jon Surrey-Dixon, Betty?"

Betty beamed serenely. "Oh, Joyce, it's wonderful! I just adore Jon; you know that."

"There couldn't be two people more perfectly matched in all the world," Joyce nodded. "I knew it the minute the two of you met."

Suddenly nostalgic, Betty thought back to her early days at OMI. She recalled her first meeting with Jon. She remembered sending him—at his request—a sampling of her poetry. It had taken him six months to respond, but he had written a warm review of her work. *Love me, love my poetry,* Betty mused with a faint smile. Then all at once, for some reason, she felt like crying. *Must be PMS,* she told herself.

Joyce never missed a thing. "Betty! What's wrong? Why the tears?" Joyce was a tiny Hispanic woman and severely crippled with rheumatoid arthritis. Her long years of suffering had made her extremely sensitive to others. She reached a pain-twisted hand toward Betty's and patted it gently.

Betty stiffened slightly. "Oh, no, Joyce. Nothing's wrong. I'm just so glad to see you that I guess I'm feeling a little emotional. Everything's wonderful. Really."

Joyce hadn't been born yesterday and looked at Betty very carefully. Was it her imagination, or was something amiss? There was no light in her friend's smile. She had lost a little weight, and the circles under her eyes, although carefully obscured with makeup, were still faintly purple.

"So tell me everything you're doing. I mean your writing and all."

"Well, I guess the biggest thing coming up is that trip to Kiev I'm supposed to make for Ed Kramer. You know about that, don't you? Jim's kind of involved."

"I heard that you and Jon were going to be working together on another book. I'm glad, because you work so well together. You express in words everything he captures with his camera. It's as if you have one mind."

Like a pale fog, sadness settled across Betty's face, and Joyce saw it immediately. "I wish Jon and I *were* doing the book together. In fact, that's why I got involved in the first place. I'm like you—I think we complement each other perfectly. But Mr. Kramer has a son-in-law who wants to be a professional photographer, and since Kramer's paying the bills he can have anybody he wants take the shots."

"Was Jon disappointed?"

"He's not as disappointed as I am. He's all excited about this Yukon expedition with a *National Geographic* team. I guess I always wanted to work together with him, but he doesn't . . . it's just not meant to be—at least not for now."

"Did you consider backing out of the project yourself?"

"I did—I was confused about my role, Joyce. A few months ago I thought God gave me a Scripture that said He would establish the works of my hands. You probably know it—it's in the Psalms somewhere. Anyway, I felt like He was saying that my writing was for Him, and that He would use it to help people. It wasn't just a job; it was a calling. So I was looking at the Kiev book as a way of helping kids. Some of those Chernobyl kids are dying, and others are going to suffer all their lives from the effects of the radiation."

"I can see your point. Jon's gone a lot anyway, isn't he?"

"Yes." Betty's voice was almost inaudible. She nodded and glanced out the window. There was a break in the conversation while Joyce studied Betty's pretty face. Yes, something was definitely wrong. She breathed a silent prayer.

"Betty . . ."

Betty turned and looked at her friend. It was no use trying to hide from Joyce. Joyce *always* knew. Hot tears spilled across her cheeks. "Oh Joyce . . ." a sob caught in her throat.

"What is it? Are you fighting? Is he unkind to you? What's happened? You love each other so much!"

Betty couldn't respond, partly because she was choked with tears and partly because she didn't know the answer. She just shook her head and gently squeezed Joyce's fingers. Finally she murmured, "He's not unkind . . . and we're not fighting."

"Betty, you are so precious . . . you don't have to tell me anything. Go get me a Bible, darling. I want to read something to you."

Betty walked into her room and took the opportunity to wipe her eyes with a wad of tissue. She removed the black mascara smudges and smears and took several deep breaths. *What is wrong with me? I'm losing it . . .* She headed back into the living room and realized she'd forgotten the Bible. Heading back to get it, she reprimanded herself as she went. *Get a grip, Betty.*

She sat at Joyce's side, wondering what verses she was about to hear. Would it be about wives learning to love their husbands? She already loved her husband—maybe a little too much. Would it be about dressing modestly, or being submissive, or maybe about being the perfect Proverbs 31 woman? She'd heard that one enough times to last a lifetime or two.

Joyce pulled her reading glasses out of her purse, perched them on her nose, and clumsily thumbed through the pages until she reached the Book of Isaiah. She began to read,

Fear not, for I have redeemed you;
I have summoned you by name; you are mine.
When you pass through the waters,
  I will be with you;
and when you pass through the rivers,
  they will not sweep over you.
When you walk through the fire,
  you will not be burned;
  the flames will not set you ablaze.
For I am the LORD, your God, . . . your Savior.

Betty looked at Joyce in bewilderment. "That's beautiful, Joyce. But why did you read it? What are you saying to me?"

"Betty, I'm not sure why I'm saying this—maybe it's God, or maybe I'm just feeling something myself. But my sense is that you are going through a time of testing, and it isn't over yet. In fact it's hardly begun."

Betty made a face. *Thanks for the encouragement. I'm not sure I want to hear any more, if you don't mind.* "What do you mean?"

Joyce continued. "I believe God brought you and Jon together. Some people get married for human reasons, but I believe you and Jon were God's specific choice to be man and wife. It's not surprising that you're struggling with things. The enemy of our souls hates for two of God's people to marry each other. They pray together with too much power, and their minds are in too much agreement. He'll keep them apart every way he can before they're married, and he'll try to come between them afterward. He'll use misunderstandings, lies, anger, hurt, sexual barriers, and temptations—any tactic he can think of—to keep them from having unity.

"You've got to pray against that, Betty. And remember this Scripture—it's in Isaiah 43. It came to me out of nowhere while we were talking, when you started to cry. Betty, child . . ."

Betty was crying again—in earnest. More scalding tears, more streaking mascara.

As best she could, Joyce put her arms around Betty and held her closely against her frail body. "You need to think about what the verses say, Betty. The Lord is promising you that no matter how difficult things get, you won't be drowned or burned or destroyed. You and Jon are going to make it through, child. And your marriage is going to be stronger than ever. Be encouraged!"

Betty's reservoir of tears spilled out for several minutes. Finally, her face swollen and streaked, she lifted her head.

"He won't talk to me, Joyce."

"At all?" Joyce found Betty's statement rather hard to believe. "I've never known a couple that enjoyed conversation as much as you two. What do you mean, he won't talk to you? About what?"

Betty shook her head sadly. "About . . . his ex-wife has been calling. She asked him to see her therapist several times, and he went. He won't tell me anything about it. I'm afraid he's still in love with her."

"That's not true, Betty. You know he's in love with you. Everybody knows that—it's written all over him. What does he say?"

"He says he loves me, and that's all I need to know."

"Why don't you believe him?"

"Because I think he's hiding something."

"Maybe he's trying to protect you from her. From what I've heard, she's quite a handful."

"I guess I just feel like an outsider. Like he doesn't trust me. I keep wondering how much he loved her when they were first married. And he's all excited about this Yukon thing—it's like going with me to Kiev was nothing to him. It's Yukon this and Yukon that. I feel so left out."

Joyce brushed a strand of Betty's hair back from her damp face. There was so much she wanted to say. She felt like presenting an on-the-spot symposium about marriage communications, followed by a quick how-to seminar on keeping emotions in their proper perspective. Instead she said, "I know how disappointed you feel right now, Betty. But if you'll ask God for wisdom, He'll show you what you can change . . ."

"Jon's the one that needs to change, Joyce. He's the one that won't talk to me."

"Are you talking to him?"

"Yeah . . ."

"Are you treating him just the way you always did? Or are you keeping him at arm's length because of his ex-wife?"

Betty knew she wasn't being perfectly honest with Joyce, and Joyce knew it, too. But she shook her head innocently, "No, I don't think I'm acting any differently. Well, maybe once in a while. But we're still in love, Joyce."

"Of course you're still in love! You two have a very special love and I don't think it's going to die easily. But treat it with respect, child. It's a gift from God, and it shouldn't be taken lightly. Let's pray for a minute before those guys get back."

Joyce took Betty's hand in hers. She spoke to heaven with a quiet authority and confidence that had come through years of intercession.

"Lord, You know more about the heartache that's come to this home than I do. I just pray that You will carry these two dear people through in Your arms. Keep them from damaging their love for each other with bitterness or resentment. Guard their hearts, Lord.

"When the waters rise, keep them from drowning.

"When the fire burns, keep them from being scorched.

"Protect them, Father. They belong to You, and I know in my heart that their love for each other came directly from Your hand. Keep these two beloved children of Yours bound together with cords of love—Your love.

"And, please, Lord. Don't let anything or anybody come between them.

"In Jesus' name, amen."

4

An F-18 Hornet screamed across the sky with terrifying sound and speed. Just as everyone on the ground began to breathe again, two identical jets, glistening blue and yellow, shrieked toward them from the opposite direction. Jon and Betty were staring into the scorching sun, their faces burned, their eyes searching the sky for more noisy surprises.

The El Toro Marine Air Station Airshow was a local attraction. It was a cross between a military salute and an aviation sideshow. Now that they were South Orange County residents, the Surrey-Dixons joined half a million other spectators to watch, among dozens of other stirring performances, the U.S. Navy Blue Angels flying in death-defying formation.

It was a spectacular California Saturday, not a cloud to be seen, not a breath of wind to disturb the colorful assemblage of shorts-clad onlookers, static-aircraft displays, snack bars, vendors, and an endless supply of aeronautical oddities. Jon and Betty were entranced by the afternoon's ceaseless attractions. The airshow created a holiday atmosphere. It was clear that the crowd had left their troubles behind—with the exception of several mothers, whose frightened, whimpering children wailed in horror every time a jet flew by.

Being a parent is a nasty job, but somebody has to do it. Fortunately it's not me, Betty thought, watching a young woman try to gladden two sunscreen-lathered children with an endless supply of Twinkies and Cokes. For the time being, Betty's compassion for children ended with orphans in foreign lands and with the thought that a stray child might somehow find its way into her household and never leave. In her self-absorbed state, such an intrusion was a chilling possibility, and she had taken every precaution to prevent its happening. She and Jon had barely mentioned having a family, and then only in the context of "later—much later."

Just the day before they had purchased their dream car—a silver-green Alfa Romeo sports car, a two-seater. Both of them had longed for a convertible, and they finally agreed to get rid of their boring Audi and have some fun. Looking forward to an outing in the shiny, new vehicle they had set the alarm for six o'clock, packed a cooler, and loaded the Alfa's "back seat." Then, with great relish, they had fired up the engine, put the top down, and driven off toward El Toro.

As gloomy as Joyce's long-range predictions had seemed during her conversation with Betty several weeks before, her prayer appeared to have been answered almost immediately. Betty had somehow let go of her worries. Curiously, after voicing her woes to Joyce, they had seemed less threatening. Perhaps she had been overreacting. In all honesty, Jon really hadn't changed in his treatment of her, ever, at all. She was apparently the one with the problem.

The calls from Carla still came sporadically. But Jon was no longer driving to the Valley to see her or the therapist. He hadn't mentioned Carla in weeks, and, when the phone rang, Betty and Jon simply exchanged exasperated looks. He assumed Betty was at peace with Carla's trespasses. She assumed he knew how upsetting the calls were and that he would put a stop to them eventually.

His Yukon trip was supposed to begin the following Friday, and neither of them was looking forward to the separation. As they rode home from the airshow, the wind whipping at them, a sense of well-being masked any worries either of them might have had about the impending time apart.

"Betty, I want to take you out Wednesday night. We'll have a little farewell dinner at the Five Crowns or anyplace you'd like to go. I'm going to have to miss our first wedding anniversary, so let's celebrate that, too. But no presents—I want to give you something later, when I get back."

"You're right, it's almost our anniversary! Can you believe it's been nearly a year? I'd love to celebrate—I love the Five Crowns!" Betty was trying to capture her hair in a baseball-style cap she'd bought from an airshow vendor. The windblown mass of long, blonde tangles wasn't cooperating. "Why not Thursday night?"

"Oh, I'll be trying to get my stuff together, and I'll need to get to bed early. It'll be my last decent night's sleep for a month."

Betty nodded. Jon and his team were going to be living in tents, seriously roughing it in the Yukon. They would be observing wildlife, photographing it, and documenting its habits and habitat. They wanted to be as unobtrusive as possible. No cellular phones, no motor homes, no radios. They would carry their supplies and try to blend in with the surroundings for three weeks.

"That makes sense. You'd better take two or three showers on Thursday, too. Because there won't be any more after that."

Jon shook his head and laughed. "I've got to be crazy to want to do this. It's going to be more torture than anything else."

"Oh, stop it. You know very well why you're going. It's one of those macho male rituals. You guys couldn't care less about wildlife. You're going out there to get in touch with the wild animal within."

Jon laughed again, thoroughly enjoying himself. "You're enough to keep me in touch with the animal within, Betty. By the way, what's happening with that Kiev project, anyway? You haven't mentioned it in weeks."

"I know. I'm half-wishing it would happen while you're gone to the Yukon. That way I wouldn't be sitting at home, waiting for you."

"Any idea when it might get under way? Have you heard from Kramer?"

Once again, uncomfortable feelings about the Kiev book arose. "That man is so weird, Jon. He called about a month ago and told me that he's still waiting for some check to come in. As much money as he has, you'd think he could afford to finance the trip whenever he wants."

"Oh, he's probably trying to juggle his books somehow. Anyhow, if you have to go while I'm gone, leave me a note and let me know where you'll be, how to reach you, and all that. I'm not sure, but I have a feeling communications from the Ukraine to here may be a little tricky, so don't worry if you don't hear from me."

Betty was completely sincere when she answered, "I'm not going to worry, Jon. I know you love me." That was exactly the way she felt—right then. As the busy days following the airshow unfolded, she lavished Jon with attention and affection. But simultaneously, her confidence began to erode ever so slightly. Jon, of course, had a lot on his mind. He was completely preoccupied with his preparations.

To make matters worse, Carla started calling every night. Betty suspected that Jon had told her he was leaving and that she was trying to get in her two cents' worth before his departure. What was Carla saying to him? Was he talking to her at other times, when Betty wasn't around?

Tuesday night another call came, and Jon answered in his now-familiar monosyllables. "Was that Carla?" Betty asked, ever so courageously.

"Yeah."

"What did she want?"

"The usual."

Quite unexpectedly, Betty's temper flared. "Jon, just exactly what is 'the usual'?" Her voice was sharp and rather accusatory.

Jon, who had been trying to balance a thousand different things in his mind all week, was in no mood for a discussion about Carla. And the tone of Betty's question made him feel defensive. "Betty, just leave it, okay? I've told you enough times not to worry about it."

"Well, I *am* worried about it, whether you think I should be or not! You're keeping something from me, and I don't appreciate it."

"I'm keeping the whole thing from you because it's none of your damned business!" Fire flashed in Jon's eyes. With that unforeseen outburst, he blasted the front door open and shut and thundered down the stairs. Betty heard the roar of the car engine and Jon peeled rubber as he drove away.

The phone rang.

"Hello?" Betty was half-thinking it was Joyce and half-hoping it wasn't.

There was a pause. And a click.

Enraged, Betty yanked the phone off the wall and threw it on the floor. The case cracked. "Good!" she shouted at the battered telephone. "I hope you're broken. I hope you never work again. I hate you! You're ruining my life!"

When Jon returned, without a word, he reconnected the phone and taped the case together. As a matter of fact, he didn't say another thing to Betty all evening. Nor did she attempt to break the silence.

Wednesday morning, they drank coffee, took showers, and got dressed without conversation. However, in the course of her entire life, Betty had never been successful at keeping her anger consciously hot for more than a few hours. She finally went over to him and kissed his cheek.

"I'm sorry, Jon," she whispered meekly.

He nodded and hugged her back. "Me too. I'll be back later on this afternoon. I have to go to Westwood to pick up some camera equipment and meet with some of the guys. We have a reservation at the Five Crowns at seven. I'll be here at about six."

"I love you!" she said brightly.

"Love you, too," he answered automatically, his lips brushing hers quickly as he left. She had the distinct feeling that he was still upset about her tirade the night before. Well, she'd said "I'm sorry." What more could she do? If she tried to explain herself, the whole thing would start all over again. She sighed, finished putting on her makeup, and walked over to her closet, wondering what she should wear for their special evening out.

The green one. He likes me in green . . . She pulled a silky, two-piece tunic dress from the back of the closet, shook it out, and hung it on a hook. *I'll wear those sparkly earrings he bought me. Maybe I'll get my nails done, too. After all, it's our first anniversary, and he's going away for a month. I want him to remember me looking my best.*

She called a local beauty salon and scheduled a manicure. Jon had taken the Alfa to Westwood, so she drove his old Mustang to the appointment. The radio was broken, the speedometer hadn't worked in years, but the car had a well-tuned V-8 engine. On that particular day, the feeling of power was especially appealing to Betty, and she broke the speed limit every chance she got.

After having her nails done, she decided to buy some green eye shadow to match her dress. That took her to the Fashion Island Mall, where she wandered around in a hypnotic stupor for a couple of hours, mesmerized by the fashionable display windows, outdoor cafes, and piped-in classical music. After restoring her senses with a café latte, she bought a sentimental anniversary card, then headed home and started to get ready for their evening out.

She and Jon hadn't had a real "date" for ages. Even though it was a farewell party, too, she was looking forward to it and the romantic interlude that would surely follow. In anticipation, she had purchased a rather seductive nightgown at Victoria's Secret.

Once she was home, Betty ironed her dress, took special care with her hair, added another coat of clear polish to her nails, sprayed herself with cologne, and finally stood admiring her reflection in the mirror. *Not bad*, she smiled. In fact she was perfect. She glanced at the clock. It was five minutes to six. The phone rang.

"Betty? Hi, it's me."

"Jon! You're supposed to be home. Where are you?"

"I'm sorry, Sweetheart. I'm still in Westwood . . . and I'm going to be here for several more hours. There was a problem at the camera store; they're waiting for a messenger to bring a couple of lenses from their Hollywood branch. But the real problem is with the guys I'm meeting with. They've made several changes in our plans."

"Jon, you're going to be with those guys for a month! We've got one more day together! Can't you just talk to them on the plane?"

"It's not that simple, Betty. Two of the men involved in this project aren't actually going. They're researchers at UCLA, and we have to get some materials from them before we leave. I'm sorry."

You're paying me back for asking about Carla, aren't you?

"Jon, what about our anniversary? This is our anniversary dinner. I'm all ready to go!"

"Oh, Betty . . ." He sounded genuinely apologetic, but she could tell he was in a hurry to get off the phone. "I'm so sorry. I didn't mean to disappoint you. Maybe we can go tomorrow night. Anyway, I've got to run. I'll see you later."

Numb and feeling a little sick to her stomach, Betty methodically took off her dress and hung it up. She removed her earrings, placing them carefully in her jewelry case. She washed off her makeup, green eye shadow and all, put on a friendly old bathrobe, and sat down in the living room, staring for hours at the cold, ash-filled fireplace.

Jon hadn't returned by ten, when exhaustion finally overtook her. Before turning out the lights, she wrote a brief statement in her journal.

Another day of waiting
'Til disappointment came
To cut the soul
To scar the heart.
But who is there to blame?

Having recorded that dismal observation, Betty checked the locks, turned on the porch light, and climbed wearily into bed. She was wearing an old sweatshirt and a pair of track shorts. The Victoria's Secret nightgown had been stuffed into the top drawer of her bureau. Hidden underneath her lingerie with the anniversary card, it was still in its bag, wrapped discreetly in tissue paper.

Friday afternoon the Surrey-Dixons drove to the airport in silence. No dinner at the Five Crowns had warmed the chilly atmosphere between them. They had tacitly agreed not to go out to eat at all, since neither of them felt like celebrating anything. Not only had Jon arrived home well after midnight, but Carla had somehow managed to call three times during the course of the day.

As always, Jon had answered enigmatically. Nothing was unusual about the calls, except that there were more of them than usual. But Betty was lost in thick, black clouds of depression. Unbridled, catastrophic thoughts were surging wildly through her mind.

Jon didn't love her.

Jon was sorry he'd married her.

Jon hated her and wished he were still married to Carla.

Jon was glad to be leaving her.

Jon cared more about going to the Yukon with a bunch of guys than he did about her feelings or their anniversary.

As for him, he was trying to focus on a multitude of professional details. Meanwhile, he wondered what he could say or do to make Betty feel better. He knew she was hurt and angry, and his late night in Westwood hadn't helped his cause. He sighed wearily. What a great way to start out on the assignment of his dreams. There wasn't a thing he could say to make things better, and now they wouldn't be able to talk for a month.

Once his luggage was checked in, which was quite an undertaking, he and Betty stood awkwardly at the gate. He glanced at her impassive face. The thought passed through his mind that he really didn't know her. He was completely inexperienced at dealing with her on an emotional level, beyond the pleasant demands of love and passion. This was new and forbidding territory. Who was this silent stranger with these cold, averted eyes?

"Betty, I love you." The words sounded trite and stilted. *What a stupid thing to say!* Jon chastised himself for being so predictable, but he was in a quandary. The more he tried to figure out how to reach out to her, the more awkward he became. "There's nothing to worry about with Carla."

She nodded, obviously unconvinced.

"I wish I were going with you to Kiev."

Betty recoiled in disbelief. Carla's sarcastic comment echoed in her mind. "Oh, so he's still a traveling man. Some things never change." *You do not! You can't wait to get on that plane and leave me. Be honest, Jon. You've thought of nothing but this trip for months. You couldn't care less about going to Kiev with me, or anywhere else for that matter!*

"I wish you were, too," Betty answered coolly. With

that, she picked up her purse and kissed Jon on the cheek. "I love you, too, but I don't understand what's happening between us."

"Betty, I want to be with you . . ."

Oh, get real! If you wanted to be with me, you'd be with me! Don't add insult to injury by lying to me!

Her body was rigid, her arms folded in front of her chest. "Do you really?"

"Of course! I . . . just have to go, that's all."

"Well, you just have yourself a *wonderful* trip, Jon. I hope you find whatever it is you're looking for out there."

His face was ashen. His hand was ice cold as he reached for her, trying to hold her arm. She pulled away. "Good-bye, Jon."

"Betty . . . please wait!"

She never heard him. The public address system interrupted, announcing that his Alaska Airlines flight to Anchorage was boarding.

Stunned to the point of feeling physically bruised, Mr. and Mrs. Jon Surrey-Dixon parted for what would amount to at least a month's time. In different sequences of thought and with various words and images, each of them wondered just how troubled their marriage really was.

Betty hadn't been in the house more than five minutes when the phone rang. *It's probably that . . .*

"Hello?"

"Betty, it's Jon. I'm calling from the plane. Listen, I want to talk to you about everything. Are you going to be home tonight?"

Of course I'm going to be home. Where else would I be going? "I don't know."

"Can I call you back when I get into Anchorage? I want to talk to you some more about this whole mess. It's just a big misunderstanding, Betty."

"What time do you want to call?"

"It has to be tonight. We leave before daybreak tomorrow for Dawson, and I won't be able to reach you after that."

"I . . . I'll try to be home."

Betty stayed home all evening. She never left the house. With growing indignation, she waited for the phone to ring. Nine. Nine-thirty. Ten. Ten-thirty. Eleven . . . All night Betty rolled around in bed, sleeping only for minutes at a time. Jon's call never came.

When she got up the next morning, Betty picked up the receiver to call Joyce. The line was dead. She checked the other receiver. It was off the hook. Somehow the kitchen extension hadn't been hung up properly.

How could I do that? Did I do it subconsciously because I'm afraid to talk to him? He must think I was avoiding him on purpose. Oh, God. How could that happen?

So maybe Jon had tried to reach her and maybe he hadn't. It no longer mattered, because whatever he had to say to her would have to wait. As for Betty, she scribbled and scratched on a legal pad until her thoughts appeared before her in all their judgmentalism and disillusionment.

> Tangled in the web of your dishonesty,
> I tremble when the wind of truth blows;
> Warm, fragrant with promise
> and oh, so lovely.
> You are enmeshed in lies, beloved.
> And I can no longer see myself
> In your clear, blue eyes.

In a cheerless Anchorage hotel room, Jon lay on a sagging bed and stared blankly at the ceiling. His thoughts

were rather unlikely ones, considering the bleak surroundings. He had been transported to Hanalei Bay. He
was holding the hand of the most beautiful woman he
had ever known. The air was warm and fragrant, and her
smile made him feel alive.

They were walking along the beach, and he was washing off a pink seashell . . .

Suddenly his eyes brimmed. He sat up abruptly,
rubbed his face with his hands, and ran his fingers compulsively through his hair. "Oh, God . . . ," he sighed.

Why had the phone been busy all night? Who could
she possibly be talking to? Had she taken it off the hook,
refusing to even speak to him? Was she that angry? That
close to the end?

He tried to reconstruct the erosion of their happiness.
It had most certainly begun with Carla's phone calls.
Wretched Carla! If Betty only knew half of it! He'd clearly
made a mistake in not telling her everything. The wild,
histrionic scenes. The violence he had endured in the
home. More recently, the threats of violence, not only
against himself, but against Betty as well.

Carla's psychiatrist had confined her to a mental health
facility months before, and although she was still managing to use the pay phone from time to time to harass
Jon, the danger of her getting out, locating their apartment, and confronting Betty was nonexistent. The
institution was like a safe, and several therapists had
assured Jon that there was no danger of escape.

When Jon had asked Betty if they could talk that night,
he had fully intended to fill her in on the sordid details.
That way her suspicions about Carla would be settled
once and for all. At this point, he preferred that she experience genuine fear rather than wallow in false
presumptions.

She thought Carla wanted him back! What a joke. More accurately, Carla wanted him dead, or at least she said she did. Hearing her repeated desires for revenge was convincing enough for him, even though her therapist claimed privately that it was "sound and fury, signifying nothing."

"That's easy for you to say," Jon had reminded the good doctor.

If I could only have reached Betty, I'd feel so much better about leaving. God, why do these things have to happen? We were so happy . . .

Again his eyes brimmed. He stumbled into the bathroom and splashed his face with the bitterly cold tap water. "Oh, God!" he groaned again. "What am I doing here? I'm thousands of miles away from the woman I love, and I'm about to lose her! How did things ever get this messed up?"

Jon sat on the edge of the bed, rubbing the back of his aching neck. In four hours, he would be checking out of this flea-bag hotel and heading for the great outdoors. Instead of his usual ardor for a coming adventure, he was weary and disinterested. So what if he was going to the Yukon? Big deal. It might look good on his resumé, but it didn't feel good. Not now. Not at all.

"Look, God. I'm sorry. Maybe it was too important to me. Maybe I had my priorities all wrong. But I thought she was going to Kiev. And I guess I thought that's what she wanted."

Jon muttered rambling prayers under his breath, rather uncertain that they were reaching the water-stained ceiling, much less any celestial realms beyond. God had seemed more real to him in his pathetic Beirut basement than He had in Southern California over the last six weeks. *No atheists in the trenches*, he reminded himself, reaching for the Gideon Bible.

Wearily he opened it and thumbed through the pages absently. If God wanted to say something, He was more than welcome to do so. But at this hour of the night, it had better be clear and direct. No metaphors, please. It was too late, and he was too depressed to figure anything out.

He flipped through Psalms, Proverbs, the Gospels, Romans. Nothing. Nothing made any sense to him. Maybe God was partial to the Middle East and didn't do house calls in the far north. Not after midnight, anyway.

He shook the book in frustration. "What is it, God? Just give me something . . ."

Flipping through the pages, he was about to give up when his eyes fixed on a verse in the Old Testament. Some words caught his attention. He read softly, "I will give them singleness of heart and action, so that they will always fear me for their own good and the good of their children after them."

Jon silently contemplated the words. Why had they caught his attention? They had nothing to do with marriage, in fact they were tied to some momentous prophecy about ancient Israel. And yet, their forthright promise of unity somehow struck him and even sounded relevant.

He and Betty had anything but one heart and one way at the moment. What they had was a major problem. He had tried to defuse a potential explosion from either woman with his "Uh-huh . . . Oh, I see . . . No . . . Yeah" responses to Carla's harangues. His clever tactic had backfired because his beloved Betty thought he was hiding something. He sighed heavily and crawled between the frigid sheets, hoping he wouldn't be sharing the bedding with any other living things.

"God," he whispered, "if we ever get things back on track, I'll be more honest. So what if she's scared? Or hurt?

Why am I protecting her from the truth? Maybe she'd better learn to live with it . . ."

He rolled over, shivered a couple of times, and finally fell into a restless sleep. Morning came quickly, and with it all communication with the world at large ended—phones, faxes, radios, and mail delivery. It occurred to him, just as their four-wheel-drive truck headed out, that if God was going to give them one heart and one way, He was going to have to do so without benefit of love letters, flowers, or intimate dinners.

But then it wouldn't be the first time Jon had been cut off from Betty. Nor was it the first time he'd been in an isolated environment where God could get his full and undivided attention. He smiled in spite of himself. Maybe this was part of the plan. Maybe it was the only way the Father could get His frenetic, frustrated son to sit down, shut up, and listen.

Two weeks passed. Betty had settled into a dull routine. She got up every morning at seven, drank two cups of coffee, read the morning paper, scanned the Bible without remembering anything she read, halfheartedly offered up a list of prayers, took a shower, dressed herself, turned on her computer, and worked. Although this regimen rendered her immensely productive, she was barely eating. She was sleeping through the night only with the help of Excedrin PM. And she was completely isolated from her friends.

Now and then the phone rang. Carla—or somebody—made an occasional hang-up call. Harold Fuller rang twice to offer fatherly advice about wandering husbands, women with competitive careers, and her sure-to-fail-marriage-if-you-don't-spend-more-time-together. Naturally his words made no impact on his hardhearted daughter. Any problems she and Jon had were Jon's fault, Jon's ex-wife's fault, or Jon's clients' fault. Betty had simply loved him "not wisely, but too well." And, like Othello, she had been brutally betrayed.

An ever-changing pattern of self-pity, bitterness, anger, and grief continuously shifted, shadowlike, across the internal landscape of her soul. Being well experienced in matters of pain, she counted the present circumstances as her lot in life. She was not meant to be happy. Even on those rare occasions when she had felt joyful, it had been an illusion that inevitably evaporated beneath the hot sun of reality.

Not hearing from Jon allowed her to focus on whatever aspects of their relationship her migrant moods brought to mind. Some mornings she mourned the loss of their breathtaking, supernatural love. Later in the day, she viewed Jon as a villain who had cruelly toyed with her. In the darkness of night, he was transformed into a weak, indecisive individual whose love for her had flamed, flickered, and failed.

Only in the most transient moments did she ever think of her husband simply as Jon Surrey-Dixon, the one man who deeply and dearly loved her—always had and always would. That thought was too out of context with an array of false beliefs about herself, about the unfairness of life, and about the way things always end up.

Just as Jon's third week in the Yukon began, Betty received a long-awaited phone call from Ed Kramer in Vancouver. In his weird way, he informed her that she would be leaving for Kiev in less than a week's time and would she please fax a photocopy of her passport to him immediately? He would take care of the Ukrainian visa.

Lost in her cares and woes, Betty had almost forgotten about the Kiev trip. It troubled her only slightly that

Jon would be coming back to an empty house. On the one hand, he wouldn't care. On the other, it served him right. Only a nagging little inner voice piped up now and then, suggesting that he might feel saddened when he came through the door and found her gone.

Jon or no Jon, she threw herself into action. She was to be out of the country for three weeks. That meant she had to finish one project a week early and postpone another deadline by two weeks. Both were workable options, considering her twelve-hour workdays and her good rapport with most managing editors. She mentally coordinated an appropriate wardrobe, calling on reliable, well-traveled Jim Richards for advice about Kiev's temperature (humid), culture (casual), and washing facilities (regrettable).

Joyce phoned the day before Betty left and quickly penetrated Betty's veneer of busyness and bravado. "How did you feel when Jon left?"

"Joyce, it wasn't a very pleasant last few days together. I'm not sure I even want to talk about it."

"Still the ex-wife problem?"

"That's one thing."

"What else?"

"Well, I frankly don't appreciate the fact that he prefers spending a month with a bunch of scientists and mosquitoes instead of wanting to be with me. I don't think he has a clue about what love is or how it's supposed to work."

"I just don't believe that, Betty."

"Joyce, you're a Pollyanna. You know you are."

"Yes, I am. But I know Jon, too. And he loves you. You just don't believe it any more."

Betty paused. For weeks, even months, she hadn't actually considered the idea that Jon might really love her. It seemed incongruous at the moment. Sure, he'd said his share of soft words. And their intimate times together were indisputably tender. But maybe that was nothing more than sexual energy. Why would he turn right around and leave again and again?

"I'm glad you feel that way, Joyce. I hope it's true. But it sure doesn't seem like it to me."

"Well, I'm praying that this time apart will give you a chance to hear from the Lord. It may turn out to be the best thing that ever happened to both you and Jon."

Joyce, you are not only a Pollyanna, you're nuts. "Well, thanks for praying, Joyce. God knows we need it."

"Yes, He does know. And remember that Scripture we read, Betty? You may pass through the waters, but they won't overflow you. The fire won't burn you, either. God is your Savior. Read it again if you have time."

"I'll keep it in mind, Joyce. Thanks for being such a good friend."

When Betty hung up, Joyce closed her eyes and shook her head. *She's in trouble,* Joyce thought. *She's given up on Jon and she's barely been married to him a year. Maybe that whole hostage thing burned her out, and she's tired of struggling.*

"God," Joyce breathed the words aloud in the sanctuary of her cluttered little office, "wake her up so she remembers what a wonderful gift You've given her. Don't let her throw Jon aside. And just in case he's not doing things the way You'd like, wake him up, too. Keep the devil away from these two, Lord. I can almost smell him, prowling around, looking around for a weak spot, ready to pounce at the first opportunity.

"Protect these two precious children of Yours, Lord. They need each other more than they realize. You've got work for them to do. And I have a feeling they are about to go through some very deep waters. Or a very hot fire. Or both."

Jim Richards, who knew Joyce almost as well as she knew herself, had been standing outside her office door. He hadn't been able to discern the first few words of her prayer, but she had raised her voice toward the end and he'd picked up the essence of it. He walked in to her cubicle and closed the door.

"I didn't mean to eavesdrop, Joyce . . . ."

"Pray for Jon and Betty, Jim. They're having a bad time."

Jim hesitated, debating whether he should entrust Joyce with some very distressing information. He knew she would keep the information confidential, so he lowered his voice, "Jon told me his ex-wife has been threatening to do some sort of violence to both him and Betty. He's trying to keep Betty from finding out about it."

Joyce stared at him in absolute horror. "Jim, Betty thinks Jon's still in love with his ex-wife!"

In spite of everything, Jim howled with laughter. "In love with *her*? She's locked up in a hospital! Women!" he choked and sputtered. "How can women be so . . . so . . ."

"Wait a minute, Jim!" Joyce was incensed. "Wait just one minute! Jon hasn't been telling Betty the truth. He's been covering up the real problem, and she's smart enough to know he's hiding something. What do you mean, 'women'? The way I see it, it's a man's poor judgment that's caused this problem, not a woman's emotionalism. I'm going to call her right now, and . . ."

Jim's voice was sharp and cold. "You most certainly are not going to call her, Joyce Jiminez! You have no business breaking Jon's confidence by talking to her about Carla. That's between them, and you can't meddle."

Joyce stiffened in her wheelchair and retorted angrily, "Well, then *you'd* better tell her, Jim Richards! She's lost faith in her husband over this, and no matter how foolish that seems to you, it seems perfectly logical to her. She's *got* to be told."

"Don't you understand? It's up to Jon to tell her. Keep out of it, Joyce. But let's do this—let's agree in prayer that they'll get this misunderstanding sorted out."

"How can we pray when we aren't doing all we can to help? The Bible says if you see a brother in need . . ."

Jim stood up abruptly enough to interrupt Joyce. He glowered menacingly. She glared back at him, her brown eyes ablaze. They were at an impasse, uncharacteristically furious at each other. But despite their sharp words, they were in deep agreement, both secretly trying to figure some way to let Betty know the truth without really telling her.

As it turned out, they never got the chance.

5

Haven't you twisted me enough?
I once stood straight and tall and tough—
Not even fear could move me then.
How could I know you would begin
This tortured bending of my will?
First comes the heat and then the chill.
You bend me gently with your smile,
Then simply vanish for a while.
You push and pull and come and go,
And if you hurt me, who will know?
Lay tenderness between the lines,
A kiss, a touch: warm little signs;
Then start the silent, icy wait.
A twist of love,
A twist of hate.
This path, once smooth, has grown so rough;
Haven't you twisted me enough?

Betty smashed her pen against the table and stared out the window into dense fog where the sea should be.

Historically, her temper had never flared for more than a few minutes at a time. But this protracted hostility was something altogether different. Just hours before, Joyce and Jim's heated exchange had taken place miles away, almost as if Betty's unrelenting bitterness had infected them, too. They had left the office separately, regretful about their own unpleasantries and unclear as to what they should say or do about Betty and Jon.

Meanwhile, Betty had received word from Vancouver that her flight would leave for London, Moscow, and Kiev that evening at six o'clock, not two days later as previously planned. *The sooner, the better,* she'd thought, hanging up the phone.

She was more than happy to be leaving Laguna Beach before Jon returned. In recent days, her resentment had intensified with every passing hour; perhaps it was some unconscious device to make departing a little easier. Even so, it could be contended that she'd allowed things to go a bit too far—emotionally.

For example, in light of her resentment, she thought that the angry poem was an appropriate farewell message for Jon. Of course, leaving it for him would have seemed unkind even to the most hard-hearted spectator. But Betty reasoned—quite unreasonably—that she would avoid phony, friendly little memos when she'd been so mercilessly abused and abandoned.

On a separate sheet she scribbled, "Hotel Rus, Kiev. June 10–30." She also left a copy of her flight itinerary. She had been given no phone numbers by Ed Kramer, but she didn't bother to explain that to Jon. In fact, she didn't bother to explain anything.

Her paperwork completed to her satisfaction and with nothing further to distract her attention, she checked and rechecked her luggage, making sure she hadn't forgotten anything important. Passport.

Tickets. Electrical transformer. Coffee, sugar, and dried milk. Despite what Jim had told her about the city, she had no mental picture of Kiev. In her mind's eye, it was a mysterious montage of golden domes and blood-diseased children. No matter. The trip was sure to be an adventure, and an adventure was exactly what she needed about now.

She had scheduled a shuttle to take her to LAX. The driver knocked on the door punctually at three o'clock and carried her bags to the van. Unexpectedly, just as she turned the key in the front door lock, a panicky feeling struck her. Jon. Their marriage. The awful poem. She wasn't handling things appropriately, and in the clear light of that moment, she knew it. How could she leave this way? *I'm being vindictive, and that's not right.* She stood immobilized on the steps.

The driver restlessly tapped his foot, standing beside the van. "We'd better get goin', lady. The 405's jammed up, and you've got an international flight. Right?"

"Right . . ." She glanced at the door, then at the driver. *Too late now . . .*

The van door slid shut, enclosing her, prisonerlike. The driver made a screeching, difficult left turn onto Pacific Coast Highway and headed north. Betty turned around in the seat and took one last look behind her, feeling more afraid than sorrowful.

Poor Jon . . .

Once the lumbering British Airways jumbo jet was airborne, Betty unsuccessfully tried to divert herself by reading an inflight magazine. It was useless. Her thoughts kept finding their way back to Jon, to how he would feel when he read the verse on the table.

God, I'm sorry. I know I'm being unfair, but I don't know how to stop. Please help me—help us. We used to love each other so much . . .

For a few moments, the steely cold armor of anger that had hidden Betty's hurt for weeks was ripped away and only naked pain remained. She wept intermittently, feeling regretful and hopeless. She had really done it, hadn't she? It wasn't enough to have frozen Jon out at the airport. Now she'd added insult to injury with her cryptic note and, worst of all, that poem. A dark, spiraling expanse of past pain soon led her thoughts, funnel-like, directly into the narrow issue of self-pity and to the questions she'd asked herself nearly all her life.

What is wrong with me? Why am I always alone? Why can't somebody just love me and share my life with me?

With that familiar enigma drifting in and out of her consciousness, she fell asleep, putting an end to her merciful mood. Once awake, she felt a good deal less apologetic about everything. So what if she hurt Jon's feelings? At least she was being honest. That was more than she could say for him! Meanwhile, she had work to do. The children of Chernobyl needed her. Ed Kramer was counting on her. And the mysterious world of Ukraine awaited her.

Lord, she prayed, almost flippantly, *work all this out, okay? Teach him a lesson.* Then, strictly as an afterthought, she self-righteously added, *and if I need to learn anything from all this, You can teach me, too. But now that I'm on my way, give me a safe trip. And while You're at it, let me have some fun. I'm tired of being unhappy.*

The trip from London to Moscow was fairly uneventful. The noisy, oddly designed Aeroflot aircraft she'd boarded at Heathrow Airport was unlike anything Betty had ever seen before, and her curiosity was piqued when the few flight attendants on board disappeared every few minutes. They came and went down a flight of stairs located in the center of the plane. Where were they going? Were they having a party down there? Or sleeping? Whatever they were doing improved neither their manners nor the quality of their service. Betty was relieved when the flight finally touched down at Moscow's Sheremetyevo International Airport.

From there she would have to find her way to Vnukovo Airport, a smaller terminal serving various Russian cities and the other republics within the borders of the former Soviet Union. Mr. Kramer had regretfully informed her that she would have to make her way to Kiev on her own; no one was able to get into Moscow to meet her flight.

In Jon's absence, Jim Richards had become Betty's travel adviser. And Jim hadn't been at all impressed with Kramer's inattention to the matters of airports and connecting flights.

"Sheremetyevo is a nightmare, especially for a woman traveling by herself. This is what you do: Look for an Intourist sign and talk only to one of their representatives. Don't speak to anybody else. And don't be afraid to pay top dollar for whatever taxi Intourist finds for you—it's Kramer's money anyway, and he can well afford it. It's ridiculous for him to send you there alone! It's dangerous, inconsiderate, and irresponsible."

"Thanks for the encouragement, Jim." In spite of his grim commentary, Betty had laughed at her friend's diatribe.

"Betty, I'm not kidding!"

"I know you aren't. You're just upset with Kramer. And he's weird. No question about it."

"Betty, it's not his weirdness that's bothering me right now. I wouldn't leave my worst female enemy on her own at Sheremetyevo—even if I honestly hated her."

"Kramer doesn't have much choice, does he? He doesn't know anyone in Moscow."

Jim had shaken his head in frustration. "Just don't go anywhere with one of those crazy taxi hustlers. They're everywhere and they're desperate for hard currency. They'd just as soon kill you as look at you. Keep your handbag safe and find the Intourist representative. Got it?"

"Got it, Jim. The Intourist rep. Honest. I really am listening."

Now on the ground in Moscow, Betty was following Jim's advice implicitly, praying constantly under her breath that God would deliver her and her luggage from the assortment of oily-looking characters bellowing "Taxi? Taxi?" directly into her face. A broad-faced blonde Intourist woman finally rescued her, leading her to a vehicle and making sure her bags got locked in the trunk.

"Fifty dollar," the woman demanded.

Without debate, Betty shoved a fifty-dollar bill in her hand. *Getting out of that pit alive was worth a hundred dollars. Thanks, God,* she sighed as the filthy car pulled onto the highway. The cab reeked of tobacco, the driver of something unspeakable he'd eaten. Nevertheless, she was safely on her way.

Through the taxicab's streaked windows, Betty watched a monotonous landscape roll by, occasionally punctuated by a drab apartment structure or a bilingual billboard. Neither item was designed with aesthetics in mind. Soviet philosophy had precluded any attention to beauty or elegance.

So much for Dr. Zhivago, Betty thought, recalling the spectacular scenery of the David Lean epic.

Here in the real world she would have to settle for gray industrial complexes and military vehicles rumbling along the highway. Determined to be captivated, however, Betty noted that the Cyrillic lettering on various signs was intriguing and that the warm breeze streaming through the driver's window was lifting her hair away from her hot, sticky face.

I wish Jon were here . . .

The thought came from a faraway place in her heart and pierced her painfully. Would Jon have allowed her to come here alone if he'd realized how difficult the journey would be? He was no stranger to Russia and knew all about the perils. Like Jim, he would have insisted that someone meet her flight, help her with her luggage, and escort her to her Kiev flight.

But Jon had *not* been there. Jon had left her on her own.

Like a pot of thick porridge, bitterness bubbled and popped sticky, hot thoughts up into her consciousness. If Jon had wanted to be with her, he would have been. He didn't care. He wasn't there. Simple facts. Case closed. Somehow Betty had forgotten that it had been her decision to take on the Kiev assignment without Jon. He had agreed, perhaps too quickly. But it was Betty who had made the choice.

The cab pulled into a gravel driveway. They had arrived at Vnukovo, whose terminal was a squalid, grimy affair. For some reason, the touching airport scene from *Casablanca* came to mind. *Bogie and Bergman wouldn't have been caught dead here, war or no war.* Betty was immediately convinced that no romantic scenes had ever been acted out on the tarmac of Vnukovo. It was impossible.

Dozens of Aeroflot aircraft were lined up behind the building. Inside, clusters of bleary-eyed passengers huddled, speaking unfamiliar languages. Hoping they weren't talking about her, Betty went to a window manned by a plump, unsmiling matron.

"Is the Kiev flight on time?"

The woman, who appeared to be an Aeroflot employee, shrugged.

"Do you speak English?"

The woman moved her hand from side to side, as if to say, "Maybe I speak a little English, and maybe I don't."

"Kiev?" Betty tried again.

The woman pointed upstairs to a waiting area.

Resorting to sign language, Betty pointed to her watch and raised her eyebrows. "Kiev?"

The woman motioned toward a timeworn sign on the wall behind her. Flights were posted there on movable wooden slats, which clattered crazily when they moved, which was not very often. All the information was written in Russian.

Resigned, Betty handed over her Aeroflot ticket to Kiev, assuming she was supposed to check in. A tiny, adhesive symbol was stuck on it, and it was handed back to her without a word.

Betty gestured toward the luggage that was piled at her feet.

The woman shrugged again.

Well, it's every man for himself, Betty determined, concluding that it might be extremely unwise to check her bags. The shrugging woman could just as easily gather them up and take them home.

Defeated by the Aeroflot representative's utter indifference, Betty dragged her belongings up the trash-littered stairs. By now she was barely able to lift them. The ten-hour journey from Los Angeles to London, a stopover, and a four-hour flight from London to Moscow had thoroughly depleted her energy. She was numb with fatigue.

Looking around the smoky room, trying to assess any immediate threats to her person, Betty noticed a prim-looking man in a coat and tie, seated on a circular seating area. *British, I presume.* Betty summoned her courage and said, "Do you speak English?"

"A little," he answered with a smile. "I am German."

Betty nodded, relieved that he understood anything at all. "What time does the flight leave for Kiev?"

"I am going to Kiev also. We wait six hours." His face was lined with weariness.

"Six hours?" Betty almost erupted into a cataract of tears. "I thought we had only about an hour's wait."

The man nodded. "There is always delay at Vnukovo. You do not know this?"

Betty shook her head, not so much in response as in abdication. "I'm going to try to sleep. Will you wake me up if they start boarding the plane?"

The man laughed. "You will have the long sleep, I think."

Betty tried to pile her luggage on the seating area so she could guard it and snooze at the same time. She tucked one bag under her knees, wrapped the strap of another around her wrist, and put her head on the third. It was an appallingly uncomfortable arrangement. To make matters worse, just as she began to doze, a family of six arrived, including a chattering mother and father, two toddlers, and two wailing infants.

Betty opened her eyes, stretched, and tried to nap again. Just then a fight broke out across the room, and everyone was suddenly alert, braced for escalating violence. "Poles," said the German man disapprovingly. "Too much vodka."

"Are they on our flight, too?"

"Of course," the man replied, as if to say, "Where else would they be going?"

Because she had been so frightened and rushed at Sheremetyevo, Betty had not exchanged any money. And now, despite a thick wad of American greenbacks in her wallet, courtesy of Ed Kramer, she couldn't even buy herself a cup of coffee.

She eyed a primitive-looking pay phone attached to the wall. Maybe she could somehow call home. Who would she want to talk to? She tried to imagine a conversation with her father and was relieved that it was an impossibility; she had no idea how to operate the contraption and didn't have a kopek to her name.

An idea struck her. "Do you have any Russian money?" she asked the German man. "I'd like to get a cup of coffee."

"Are you sure?" he looked astonished. "This coffee is very, uh, how you say it? Awful."

Even awful coffee sounded comforting to Betty at the moment. "I'm sure you're right, but I'll try it anyway."

With a don't-say-I-didn't-warn-you look on his face, the German reached into his pocket and handed her a couple of crumpled bills.

She opened her purse. "No," the man held up his hand. "No, keep your money. Have a coffee on me. I will stay with your . . ." he motioned to the bags, unable to remember the right word.

After thanking him as lavishly as was possible under the circumstances, Betty found her way into a bleak coffee room, which consisted of a counter and several unwiped tables.

"Café?" she said to the toothless woman at the counter. Feeling suddenly daring, she pointed to a slice of black bread sitting by itself on a plate. She had no idea about the price of anything, so she shoved both bills into the woman's hand. With a reprimanding look, meant to chide Betty for such an extravagant and careless use of rubles, the Russian worker tossed one bill back, kept the other, and gave Betty several small coins.

The coffee was, as predicted, more terrible than anything Betty could have ever imagined. The cup was half filled with some sort of sludge, which must have represented several decades of brewing. However, a generous addition of sugar made it palatable, if barely so. And the black bread was sour, but pleasant, all things considered.

After her meager snack, Betty felt slightly energized. Counting on the German's promise to watch her bags, she located a malodorous restroom where she brushed her hair, replaced her lipstick, and braced herself to survive another four hours at Vnukovo Airport.

Surveying the inebriated Poles, the cacophonous family, two or three weary foreign businessmen, and an array of African students, Betty shook her head in dismay. *Welcome to the glamorous life of world travel. Move over, Richard Halliburton. I'm writing my own* Book of Marvels *now. Next stop, the arctic wastelands of Archangel—tundra specimens included in the round-trip dogsled fare.*

As fate would have it, Betty finally arrived in Kiev. By the time she got there, an entire night had passed. She arrived at Borispol, another grubby airport, early the following morning. To her immense relief, the Dunns were there to welcome her. Once she was in their company, her optimism was faintly restored.

Dr. Dunn was a sober, graying gentleman in his mid-fifties. He could be identified by his thick glasses, protruding Adam's apple, and quiet, polite manner. He was genuinely delighted that Betty had come to Kiev, and in his unobtrusive way he made every effort to make her feel welcome.

Mrs. Dunn, who immediately insisted on being called Marian, was a buxom, clear-eyed woman with salt-and-pepper hair and a ready smile. Betty could not help but notice the tranquility in Marian's face and the quiet respect she and her husband demonstrated toward each other.

It was immediately clear that Steven and Marian Dunn were facing life united—same goals, same journey, same motives. There was nothing glamorous about either of them—physical appearance obviously wasn't the secret to their relationship's success. Betty pondered the phenomenon. Maybe it was their dedication to a mission or their isolation in a foreign land that had fused them so inseparably to each other. Whatever the reason, the two had clearly become "one flesh." Whatever else transpired here, not one incident during her entire stay in Kiev contradicted Betty's first, positive impression of the Dunn's solid marital relationship.

I wish Jon could meet them . . . She stifled the thought instantly. If Jon had wanted to be here, Jon would have been here. And so on and so forth went the disavowal every time Jon's memory recurred.

"I'm sorry we had to put you in the Hotel Rus, Betty. It's not very luxurious, I'm afraid. The Intourist Hotel next door to it is much better, but Mr. Kramer specifically asked us to put you in the Rus. We'd love to have you stay with us, but as you'll soon see, there's not even room for you to sleep on the floor."

"Where are we going first?"

"Well, I can see that you're exhausted. Would you like to check into the hotel?"

"I think if I took a nap, I'd feel better. But what if I don't wake up till tonight?"

"I'll tell you what. After we get you checked into your room, we'll take you home with us so you can take a shower and have a proper meal. You can rest for a few hours in our bedroom—we'll leave you alone while we take care of some things. Then we'll come back, wake you up, and drive you out to the hospital for a sort of introductory visit."

When the Dunns' car pulled into the Hotel Rus parking area, Betty was disconcerted. *Dear God! Three weeks here?* The hotel was a rundown structure, its outside signs in need of paint and its interior in need of a good scrubbing. A cluster of swarthy, Syrian-looking men stood outside smoking. They stared at her unapologetically as she and the Dunns walked past them. Inside, several groups of unkempt males were aimlessly wandering around, waiting for something or somebody and meanwhile ogling Betty. She glanced at the Dunns. *You expect me to stay here alone?*

In fluent Russian or Ukrainian, Betty was never sure which, Steven Dunn checked her into the hotel, got the key to her room, and led the way to a bank of dilapidated elevators. The three rode in silence, Betty feeling more insecure by the moment. At least she'd be going home with the Dunns for the rest of that day. She was too weary to deal with any of this.

The elevator doors parted on the eighth floor. Directly in front of them were several dumpy chairs, a vintage television, and an unwatered house plant. A man in striped pajamas was watching television and smoking a cigar, oblivious to their arrival.

Marian squeezed her arm. "Don't worry—this is the eighth floor lounge. People are very informal here." Leaving the lolling gentleman behind, they turned down a dimly lit hallway and located Room 824. The door opened easily—too easily. Inside, there were no safety locks and no security chains.

Betty's room featured uncarpeted wooden floors, two narrow, hard beds, a desk, an unscoured bathroom, and a large, drape-covered window. It was stifling inside the room. When Steven opened the drapes and cranked open the windows, a warm wind snapped at the curtains and the smell of stale smoke began to abate.

Betty took a look outside and found herself gazing directly down into Kiev's cavernous Dinamo Stadium. *How convenient,* she noted, *in case I decide to watch a ball game in my spare time. This is just like those luxury clubhouse suites at Anaheim Stadium.*

Dr. Dunn explained the phone system and marked the important numbers on a list that was posted next to the dial telephone. Nodding mutely, Betty hoped she would remember at least something he was telling her. Fatigued by her journey and depressed by her surroundings, she couldn't think of one thing to say, except, "Thanks. I really appreciate all your help."

Finally, after hanging up her wardrobe in the cubicle that served as a closet, she picked out a change of clothes and locked the door, leaving her room behind. The Dunns sensed Betty's discomfort with the Hotel Rus. And Betty didn't want to insult them, or their adopted city, with negative comments. So down the elevator the trio went, silent and serious. As they headed for the door of the hotel, a kiosk of souvenirs caught Betty's eye.

"Oh, wait. Do you mind if I just take a quick look?"

"Of course not, Betty," Marian smiled, relieved to see that their guest wasn't permanently disinterested in all things pertaining to Kiev.

As the two women examined an unexceptional assortment of nesting dolls, enameled spoons, and amber jewelry, Steven Dunn stood by, waiting and watching the people around them. Studying the assortment of characters in the lobby level, he saw a handsome, western-looking man standing in a shadow, only a few paces away from them. Dr. Dunn couldn't help but notice that the man was watching Betty's every move.

The dark-haired gentleman was casually leaning against a wall, partly obscured by a column, drinking a beer. He was well dressed and wore a rather inscrutable smile on his face. Steven's first thought was that he would be introducing himself to Betty before many days passed. Just as he took into account the fact that she really was quite an attractive woman, Steven also remembered that she was married.

Too bad for him, Dr. Dunn concluded. *He'll be disappointed when he finds out she's unavailable.*

In actual fact, the admiring Westerner knew very well that Betty Surrey-Dixon was married. He could have reported the exact date and location of her wedding, and her husband's name, business, and history. He also knew that Betty would be staying in Kiev, at the Hotel Rus, for three weeks.

Mike Brody had been awaiting Betty's arrival for several hours. And he intended to bide his time until the optimal moment arrived for him to reintroduce himself.

Jon Surrey-Dixon sat on the rocks at the foot of the Victoria tower reading the poem again and again. A sick hollowness gnawed at his insides. Disbelief continued to whisper, "It's not meant for you." But considering Betty's frigid posture at the airport and the fact that she'd not been available for his call from Anchorage, he was quite sure the poem's message was directed toward him and him alone.

He had arrived home three hours before, spent from his journey and looking forward to a forthright conversation with his wife. The time away had served him well, both spiritually and practically, having given him opportunity to clearly see how foolish he'd been. He should have confided the truth about Carla to her right from the start. And, although the Yukon expedition had been fascinating, he'd felt removed from the other men. They'd been either single, divorced, or embittered with their wives. He had been nothing short of homesick, counting the days until he could get home.

But home for what? For this? He shook his head, rubbed his face, and ran his fingers through his hair. Was it too late? Had Betty written him off completely? While in Canada, Jon had made several decisions about their future together. Before the day was over, he was going to add a private phone line and put their existing line on an answering service. The private number would only be given to trusted friends. Carla would no longer be able to reach them, and her harassing calls would cease. Jon also intended to have a few words with her therapist regarding her incessant phone calls.

He was trying to figure out some ways he and Betty could work together. He was thinking of several book proposals they could coproduce. And he planned to introduce her to a couple of influential editors. "This is my wife Betty," he would tell them proudly, "as well as my business partner."

Jon had been exhilarated by those notions as recently as yesterday. But now he was gripped with fear.

> "This path, once smooth, has grown so rough;
> Haven't you twisted me enough?"

He searched his soul. Had he ever, even once, intended to hurt Betty? To "twist" her? To ignore her or minimize her importance? True, he had been captivated with the Yukon trip. And she had taken that rather personally, or so he suspected. But had she intended that he tag along to Kiev, to be unpaid for three weeks, while some Canadian amateur clicked his way around town with an autofocus camera? Surely she hadn't expected that. Or had she?

He thought back across the years. Betty had always been insecure when he didn't keep in close touch with her. That hadn't seemed exceptional. If anything, he had worried about her overzealous devotion to him. Well, right at the moment, he would have gladly settled for a good dose of her overzealousness.

But just how committed was she, anyway? He remembered the Mike Brody incident in Wiesbaden with no small amount of discomfort. When he'd arrived there, his skin had been still raw from the chains that had held him. He had been mentally and physically exhausted, released from captivity just hours before. Unable to put two words together, even for Betty, he had mumbled something about getting some sleep. She had left, perhaps disappointed with his unpolished performance as an ex-hostage.

That very night she had gone out for a drink with "a friend." That friend, Mike Brody, happened to be one of Jon's intelligence debriefers.

Afterwards, Jon had done some debriefing of his own. He had interrogated Betty more than once about the incident, and she had finally convinced him that it was nothing more than a casual conversation at a local hotel bar. But the possibility that she wasn't telling the whole story still rankled. Especially now. Queasy with fear and uncertainty, Jon stood up and looked at the sea.

"God," he whispered aloud, "did I really 'twist' her? Did I? I'm sorry. You know how much I love her. Oh, God

I'm so sorry. I've messed this up so badly." Emotion choked him unexpectedly. "Don't let me lose her, God. Just tell me what to do."

Get yourself to Kiev.

The thought flew across Jon's mind out of nowhere, like a rogue F-18 Hornet from another dimension. It startled him, almost leaving him breathless. *Kiev?* Jon stood staring at the Pacific Ocean, running his fingers through his hair repeatedly. "Kiev?" he repeated aloud. It seemed illogical at first. After a few moments, however, he qualified his initial response. Maybe getting himself to Kiev wasn't such a bad idea.

Shaking the sand out of his shoes and heading back up the stairs, Jon decided to call Jim Richards. *He's been married for years. Maybe he understands women . . .*

On his way up the hill to their apartment, for some reason Jon remembered the Old Testament passage he had found in Anchorage. "I will give you one heart and one way." The Surrey-Dixons were a far cry from having one heart these days. And as for one way, the only possibility for that to happen was for them to manage being in the same place at the same time.

Kiev, here I come, Jon thought grimly, wondering how long it would take to get a Ukrainian visa.

He picked up the phone the minute he got home.

"Jim? Hi. It's Jon. Yeah, I'm back."

"Hey, it's good to hear your voice, buddy."

"Jim, I've got a problem you and I need to talk about. It's . . . I hate to even admit it, Jim, but Betty and I are having some problems."

Jim fixed his eyes on Joyce, who happened to be sitting in his office at the time. He chose his words carefully. "I know things have been a little rough, Jon. Betty talked to Joyce before she left for Kiev. You know, she thinks you're still in love with Carla. At least that's what she told Joyce."

Jon was again beset with utter disbelief. First the poem and now this. His muddled emotions quickly transformed themselves into anger. "Me? In love with Carla? Jim, you know better than that! I don't know that I ever was in love with her. And I'm sure not in love with her now!" He spat out the words, so furious was his rejection of the whole idea.

"Take it easy, Jon. I know. I hear you. But Betty didn't talk to me. She talked to Joyce, and Joyce didn't know about the Carla situation. I hope you don't mind, but I told her."

"Of course I don't mind! Thank God you told her!" Jon calmed himself. "Did Joyce talk to Betty about it before she left for Kiev?"

"Never had the chance, Jon. We both wanted to . . ." Jim was staring at the ceiling. Joyce was staring at Jim, her face a study in astonishment. Was he saying what she thought he was saying? "We both wanted to"?

Men! She bristled. *They're all cowards, every last one of them. And they don't know fact from fiction!*

Jim could feel Joyce's gaze burning into him. He closed his eyes tightly and made a gesture that looked very much as if his throat were being cut. Disarmed, Joyce's annoyance abated and she chuckled in spite of herself.

"Jim," Jon was saying, "I'm thinking about flying over to Kiev to be with her. I need to talk to her, but I'm just afraid if I do, I'll say all the wrong things and cause even more trouble ."

"You're a well-spoken man, Jon. Why would you say all the wrong things?"

Jon rubbed his eyes wearily. "For as long as I can remember, something always goes wrong when I try to talk to emotional women, Jim. Even as a boy I had problems talking to my mother—she'd either scream at me or cry. It didn't take me long to learn to keep my mouth shut. And I don't have to remind you about Carla. I can talk about anything to anybody, and women don't bother me a bit when we're discussing safe subjects. But start dealing with emotions and I lose my vocabulary or, worse yet, I come up with all the wrong words."

"That's hard to believe, Jon. I've never seen you at a loss for words."

"Like I said, it only happens with women." Jon was rubbing his eyes again and running his fingers absently through his hair.

"Well, it sure casts some light on this misunderstanding you've had with Betty. So does she fly off the handle like Carla did?"

"No! Not at all. She just gets quiet and withdraws from the conversation. The trouble with Betty is figuring out what she's thinking. She won't defend herself when she's hurt or upset, so I'm always trying to read her mind. Then I get nervous and don't say what I mean. Next thing you know, we're giving each other the silent treatment."

After a brief pause, Jim quietly said, "I understand what you're saying. It sounds like you've got some explaining to do and some changes to make. I guess you'd better figure out your script before you see her again, Jon."

"Yeah, I know. I'm already rehearsing. So how long will it take me to get a visa?"

"That's an expensive trip you're talking about, isn't it? She'll be home in two and a half weeks. Why don't you just wait?"

Jon calculated for only a split second. "I can't wait. This is a serious problem. I've got two round-trip tickets to London. I'll use one of them to get to London and cash in the other one to pay for the London-Kiev connection.

"Okay, well if you're sure that's what you want to do, let me get back to you about the visa. If you go through Moscow, I think you'll need a Russian transit visa, too. I'll make a couple of calls. Do you want to talk to Joyce?"

"Sure. I'd like to say hello."

There was a pause while the receiver was passed over and Jon wasted no time on small talk. "Hi, Joyce. So Betty thinks I've stopped loving her?"

Joyce sent a prayer rocketing toward heaven and spoke very calmly. "Jon, Betty's so much in love with you, she's just afraid she's going to lose you. Sometimes I think she creates problems where there aren't any just because she can't believe she actually has you forever."

Jon tried to comprehend what Joyce was saying. "I love her very much, too. Why would she think she's going to lose me?"

"Maybe you should tell her you love her just a little more often, Jon. Reassure her. You know how women are . . ."

I'm not sure I do know, but I have a feeling I'd better find out. "Joyce, she left without saying good-bye." Jon's voice broke unexpectedly. "No note, nothing but her itinerary and a poem."

"Maybe the poem was her way of saying good-bye."

Jon shivered. Joyce's innocent comment sounded far too accurate, and he could only hope she wasn't inadvertently exercising some hitherto-unknown prophetic gift. "I hope not. God, I hope not!" With that and unable to find further words, he excused himself and hung up.

That afternoon Jon changed the Surrey-Dixon phone number. He also called Carla's psychiatrist and informed him that he was no longer available for therapy sessions or any other involvement. "I should have said no in the first place," Jon remarked crisply.

"I find that very nonsupportive," the shrink whined. "I'm sure you know by now that you have a classic passive-aggressive personality. I think it's about time you got in touch with the pain you experienced growing up in such a dysfunctional family of origin."

Jon was in no mood for lectures, particularly from one of Carla's allies. "I think it's about time I gave my full attention to my present wife," he retorted, trying very hard not to sound defensive. "And as for my past, I guess I'll deal with that in my own way on my own time. Tell you what, don't waste your concern on me. You just worry about Carla. That'll give you plenty to do. Oh, and by the way, I'd appreciate it if you'd make sure she quits calling our home. She's been harassing both me and my wife, and I've had enough of it!"

Jon felt cleansed and relieved having disengaged himself from his ex-wife and her therapist once and for all. In the process of trying to sort out his next steps, he paced around the house. He touched a plant here, a piece of furniture there. The pink seashell sat, forlorn and dusty, next to the arrangement of dried sea lavender.

"I'll never forget," they had promised each other. Barely a year had gone by and they'd both let the honeymoon enchantment slip away. Jon wandered into the bedroom. It was empty—no Betty. Wanting to feel her closeness, he opened her dresser drawers, one at a time.

Underneath some lingerie, he felt paper. He pulled out a bag marked with the Victoria's Secret logo. Inside were two items: a lace nightgown, still tagged, and an anniversary card.

"To my husband on our first anniversary," the gold script on the outside read. "Thank you for making this the best year of my life," Betty had written below the inside message.

Oh God, the dinner at the Five Crowns. She must have bought this for . . . Again he was overcome with that choking, strangling emotion.

He carefully returned the bag to the drawer. Then, having second thoughts, he pulled it out again. "If I go to Kiev, this is going with me. Better late than never."

Suddenly gripped with frustration, Jon glared into the mirror atop the bureau and raged aloud at his haggard reflection.

"You damned fool! You're losing your wife! Isn't it about time you did something about it?"

6
_____

The little girl's eyes were large and blue. As Betty held her, she noticed the pale traces of violet veins beneath her translucent skin.

"Leukemia," Dr. Dunn whispered as Betty had lifted the child onto her lap.

She remembered the beautiful African children she had visited not many years ago in a Ugandan orphanage. They had been poverty-stricken, but in the loving environment of the orphanage, most of them radiated health and happiness. Their eyes gleamed, and their friendly smiles were irrepressible.

In contrast, each of these little ones was almost transparently fragile, with porcelainlike skin and an uncertain future. A melancholy air hovered over their families. Unrelieved grief was reflected in the weary faces of their mothers, and the same hopelessness was evident in their fathers' detached formality. Without exception, sorrow had become a dominant element in each of their lives.

As Betty spoke with the various children whose stories might be featured in the book, memories of her own unhealthy childhood came to mind. Her skin disease had robbed much of the joy from her own early years. And more than one urgent hospitalization had cast the shadow of death across the Fuller family's daily existence.

There's nothing like a little déjà vu to make a bad day worse.

Ed Kramer's son-in-law had failed to arrive in Kiev. As far as anyone could determine, he might not arrive for another week or two. Some sort of personal problem had arisen, and the Dunns had received a phone call just before Betty's arrival advising them of the open-ended delay. They considered themselves fortunate to have received word at all—phone calls from outside the country came few and far between.

Betty was just as happy to start her work without him. She was convinced that he was probably a troublesome novice and, above all else, a usurper of Jon's rightful job. She felt they would both be better off if she composed her part of the book without laying eyes on him.

The Dunns had selected a dozen children who had either unusual or deeply moving stories, each depicting some aspect of the way Chernobyl's accident had affected their young lives. Some of them had lost brothers and sisters, others had seen their parents die. One little girl's father had continued to work courageously at the leaking Chernobyl facility well after the 1986 disaster. He had been offered a great deal of money to do so, and his concern for financial well-being had completely obscured his sense of self-preservation. He had died just weeks before Betty's arrival.

And so the stories went. Betty and Ed Kramer had determined that each child would be represented by a chapter in the book. Each depiction would be a variation of heartbreak, heroism, and God's love in the midst of pain. Betty would explore the children's medical histories, their families' backgrounds, their personal qualities and interests, and their hopes and fears for the future. The Dunns had done a great deal of work for her in advance, carefully organizing and preparing the documentation.

Although grim and in need of paint on the outside, the Dunns' medical facility was fairly well equipped, thanks to the efforts of several Christian ministries. Funds had been raised in a number of ways to assist the children.

"Chernobyl has been a good cause for fund raising in the West," Steven politely commented.

Marian gave Betty a meaningful look. "What he means is that it's a good chance to exploit a tragic situation. Some people, like you, come here to help, and they couldn't be more sincere. But there are some others, a few American do-gooders I could mention, who are more interested in being videotaped than they are in helping sick kids."

"I know what you mean," Betty smiled as they walked back toward the Dunns' car. "My husband was a hostage in Lebanon, and there was a television evangelist who interviewed me. When I finally saw the broadcast, I was horrified. He made it sound like Jon would be released if people would send money to his ministry. He was clever, too. His people edited the interview so that it looked like I was always crying my eyes out. I looked like a blubbering idiot."

The Dunns laughed, understanding all too well. "Tell me about your husband," Marian asked cheerfully. "How has he recovered from his ordeal?"

Betty winced. She didn't want to talk about Jon to anyone, most notably not to a psychologist. "Oh, he's doing fine."

"What kind of work does he do?"

"He's a professional photographer. He worked with me on the Ugandan book."

"Oh, of course. We'd hadn't realized he was your husband when we suggested that he do the book with you."

"Well, he wasn't my husband then. Unfortunately, at the moment he's on assignment in the Yukon."

"It really is a shame he couldn't have come with you here, isn't it? Do you get to spend much time together?"

Once again the bitter tide began to rise inside Betty. She consciously worked at keeping it from overflowing into her conversation. "I had hoped Jon could work with me here, but Mr. Kramer wanted his son-in-law to do the photography. Jon had plenty of other work to keep him busy, so he told me to come ahead without him." Betty was unconsciously fidgeting with her hands as she spoke.

"How long have you been married?"

"Just over a year," she replied glibly. "Oh, isn't that one of the famous Kiev churches?"

Marian, who depended more on intuition than her education as a counselor, glanced curiously at Betty and then at a gilded dome atop a hill. "That's not one of the better-known ones. If there's time, we'll try to give you a little tour. Do you see that statue over there? It's a very unpopular tourist attraction around here. Most people resent the fact that it towers above the churches. Even nonbelievers hate it. It's supposed to represent the Motherland, but to them it just looks like another Bolshevik monstrosity."

A massive, sword-wielding woman loomed above the city, menacing in her posture. Firmly planted on a hill above the Dnieper River, she was incontestably the most striking landmark in sight.

Betty responded enthusiastically to the conversation's change in direction. The less Marian picked up about her problems with Jon, the better. She was in no mood to discuss her personal feelings of rejection or disappointment.

Besides, Marian and Steven obviously had a storybook marriage, the kind people write self-help manuals about. Their closeness touched a deep wound in Betty's soul. Until recent months she had believed that she and Jon had a similar singleness of mind. But today that seemed like a foolish, naive illusion.

"Let me not to the marriage of true minds admit impediments . . . ," the Surrey-Dixons had quoted Shakespeare's sonnet at their wedding. Maybe it was about time Betty admitted that there were, indeed, several impediments to the marriage of their minds. But she wasn't about to admit it to Marian, professional shrink and perfect wife.

After a small meal at the Hotel Ukraine, mostly vegetables and soup, the Dunns escorted Betty to the Kiev-Perchersk monastery. An ancient Christian shrine, it was a cluster of buildings and gilded domes that represented Christianity's first inroad into Russia. It dated back more than a millenium and was rich in the elaborate artwork that typifies the Orthodox church.

Something stirred within Betty as she toured the monastery's chapels and catacombs. Beneath gleaming cupolas, inside quiet sanctuaries, slender candles illuminated an array of intricately painted icons. Garden flowers, lovingly gathered and brought as spiritual offerings, were everywhere. The life of Christ was depicted in vivid scenes, silently reminding her of His mission.

Betty stared at a huge portrait of the crucifixion. "Father, forgive them—they know not what they do." The words resounded in her mind, and for some reason she immediately thought of Jon. Compassion swelled inside her. Had he really wronged her so severely? Instinctively, she hardened herself against the charitable impulse. *Of course he knows what he's doing. How could he not know?*

But the monastery's sacredness was pervasive. It continued to nudge her, to prompt her toward lofty principles. The amber candles represented humble prayers, each one meant to reach heaven in its waxen importunity. How much had she prayed about her present plight? Not as much as she should have.

Vast, elaborate ceilings, rich in angels and heavenly sights, spoke of great, awesome feelings and eternal magnanimity. Christ had, indeed, forgiven much. How very little she had to forgive.

But Betty was not of a mind to relinquish the energy generated by her rage. It felt empowering. It gave her a sense of invincibility. So what if Jesus was forgiving? Betty had never claimed to be perfect. And she'd put up with her share of imperfect people, too, to say nothing of tears. Enough was enough.

Once they returned to the uncelestial light of the Ukrainian afternoon, Betty found herself grateful to escape the monastery's spiritually coercive atmosphere. Only one vestige of its influence remained with her. On an impulse, she had bought a crucifix crafted by the same order of monks who had first come to Kiev. It would provide a nice, religious touch to her home. Naturally Harold Fuller, her perpetually Protestant father, would hate it, a minor complication that made it all the more interesting.

In passing, it occurred to Betty as the Dunns drove her back to the Hotel Rus that her spirit had reached a rather dismal condition. She was being immensely evasive in her conversations, and she was nursing an ongoing grudge against Jon. Some unwelcome voice quietly warned her that her soul was in an unhealthy state. The thought of those cancer-ridden children came to mind, along with the thought that *unforgiveness is spiritual malignancy.* Annoyed by the thought, she hardened herself again.

Bidding the Dunns good-bye, she climbed out of the car and stalked across the parking lot, feeling quite independent and exceptional. She was barely out of earshot when Marian Dunn turned to her husband and said, "There's something wrong between her and her husband." Steven nodded gravely.

Meanwhile, as Betty strode through the doors of the Hotel Rus, a handsome, dark-haired man moved toward her. By the time she pushed the elevator button he was standing next to her.

"Betty! Is it you?" His voice was animated with surprise.

She turned and caught her breath in wonder. "Mike Brody! What are you doing in Kiev?"

The reunion was a delight. Betty was almost ecstatic to have found a friend in the unpleasant hotel. And such a friend! Her old pal Mike Brody had never failed to intrigue her. He was a mystery man who never spoke of the past or future. This, of course, limited their conversation to the people, places, and things that surrounded them and to their own fascination with each other.

Before long they were sitting in a noisy nightclub, which was simply dubbed "The Red Room," on the hotel's mezzanine level. Cigarette smoke hung in blue curtains above the candlelit tables—apparently, the dangers of tobacco had not been publicized in this part of the world. A cramped dance floor was filled with couples slowly sidestepping across the parquet.

"Mike, what are you doing here? You never told me."

"Oh, you know me. I can't tell you all the details, but I've got a little work to do here. Middle East followup. That sort of thing."

Betty's mind made a quick review of international affairs. The quiet revolution that had overthrown the old

USSR had resulted in a fragile commonwealth of former republics. Across the broad expanse, from Europe into Asia, forces of various ideological convictions swelled and diminished unpredictably. Fascists and old-line Communists tugged against each other in the north, while Islamic factions gained strength in the south.

It wasn't surprising that the CIA (or whomever Mike *really* worked for) was prowling around, checking out the territory. And it made sense that he could be following up on Middle East affairs—the hotel was packed with Syrians.

"Where are you staying? Here?"

Mike shook his head, smiling enigmatically. "I move around."

"It's just incredible that you're here, Mike. I can't get over it."

Mike laughed disarmingly. Betty would never know how carefully he'd arranged their meeting. She couldn't have guessed that he had falsified reports in order to prolong his stay in Kiev. His assignment had been finished forty-eight hours before. He was simply pursuing an obsession, and that particular obsession was completely entranced with him at the moment. "It's pretty amazing all right. I guess we're just destined to be together. By the way, how's married life treating you, Betty?"

She studied his attractive profile as he glanced away, perhaps a little shyly, after asking the question. He was such a good-looking man.

"Oh, nothing's ever perfect, Mike. You know . . ."

Mike nodded, his face soft with compassion. "I'm sorry, Betty. Did you get my letter?" Now he was looking directly into her eyes.

She remembered the letter, the crackling sound it had made in her jeans pocket, the shame she'd felt at the sight of the pink, Hawaiian shell. *I'll never forget . . .* Tears suddenly stung her eyes. *Damn you, Jon!*

Braced by her bitterness, she answered, "Yes, I did, after our honeymoon. It was nice of you, Mike. Really kind."

"I meant every word of it, you know. But tell me—what's not so perfect with married life? To be honest, I thought you and Jon would live happily ever after. What's his problem?"

"Oh, Mike, he's got this ex-wife who keeps calling. I don't know what she wants. I . . . I'm not sure . . . I almost think he's still in love with her."

Although the words hadn't found their way out of her mouth easily, Betty could hardly believe she was telling Mike anything about such a personal, painful matter. What had come over her? She had steadfastly refused to talk about her problems with Marian Dunn. So why should she spill it out to Mike? For a moment, she felt like she was betraying Jon. She stiffened, and her resolve hardened. Jon wasn't there. Mike was. No harm, no foul.

The music stopped, and their voices dropped.

"I don't know what his ex-wife is like, Betty, but she can't be as beautiful as you are." Mike's voice was so low she could hardly hear him. She very much wanted to, so she moved her head a little closer to his. Impulsively, he kissed her hair. She withdrew.

"Mike, don't . . . please."

"I'm sorry." Apologetically, Mike held up his hands. "I didn't mean to do that. I honestly didn't. You're just so . . . Look, Betty, I want you to know that I respect your marriage and that I'll never do anything to get in the way. Let's just settle that right now. But I feel bad about this ex-wife business."

"Well, she's got some problems, apparently, and her

therapist wanted Jon to come to the counseling sessions to help sort out her behavior."

Mike stared at her, aghast. "Don't tell me he went!"

"Well, yeah, he did. Now Mike, in his defense, I think he felt like he hadn't really tried to work things out with her while they were married. Once she found a lover, he filed for divorce without a word. I think his idea was to be a little more specific with her about his feelings. She's got all kinds of problems and he wants to help."

Mike was sharply critical of Jon. "Guilt or no guilt, I just can't imagine a married man doing something like that. Going into therapy with his ex-wife? No way! It's unbelievable." Mike looked genuinely appalled. Betty wondered why she hadn't recognized just how incorrect Jon's behavior had been. True, she'd resented it, but until now it hadn't seemed quite so outrageous.

The band, which was composed of bored, middle-aged players, struck up an uninspired rendition of "Lady in Red." Betty, who had always loved the song, was dressed in a crimson knit dress. Endearingly spontaneous, Mike squeezed her hand. "I don't think Jon would mind if you danced with me—just this once. Do you?"

The way things are going, I don't know what Jon would mind and what he wouldn't.

"I don't think he'd mind, either," she said, and soon she was tightly pressed against Mike's warm, strong body, caught in the magic of the song. "Lady in red . . . dancing with me . . . Nobody here, just you and me . . ."

Once the tune was over and they returned to their table, Mike abruptly asked for the check. He paid for their dinner with an untidy fan of tattered rubles and said, "We'd better go."

At first Betty wondered if she had done something wrong or said something she shouldn't have. Mike was uncharacteristically quiet as they walked out the door, down the curving stairs, and toward the wall of elevators.

"Mike, what's wrong?"

He looked at her, his eyes searching hers. "Betty, you're just too much for me."

"I'm sorry, Mike. I didn't mean to do anything . . ."

He smiled, brushed her face with the back of his hand, and whispered. "It's not what you *do*—it's what you *are*." He kissed her cheek, explained that he'd try to see her again before he left town, and headed for the front door without looking back.

Betty was completely unaware of her journey up the elevator or down the hall to Room 824. She was mesmerized, caught up in the momentum of Mike's advances. And she was nearly breathless with the marvel of his sudden appearance in Kiev, along with the distinct possibility of seeing him again.

When she entered her room, the message light was on. Betty dialed "0" to reach the operator, but got an unfamiliar signal. She searched the list of numbers Steven Dunn had marked and tried to remember his instructions. No luck. Once she'd attempted every possible combination of digits, she decided she was too tired and too distracted to go through it all again. Who would be calling anyway? Probably the Dunns, and they'd most certainly call back.

Lost in a happy haze, she locked the door, removed her red dress, and climbed into the stiff little bed. It could have been a bed of nails or a cumulus cloud, so oblivious was she to her surroundings. Rehearsing Mike's compliments and remembering his unintentional gestures of affection, she gradually drifted off into a dreamless sleep. *It's about time I had some fun*, was her last conscious thought.

Jon was encountering obstacles in every direction. He couldn't get a straight answer about his visas from the local consulates, and he couldn't purchase airline tickets into Russia or the Ukraine without a visa. To compound his problems, he ran into a huge error in the Surrey-Dixon checkbook that neither he nor the bank could comprehend.

He had finally been able to find a phone number for the Hotel Rus, but he was startled to learn that every room had a private number of its own. He didn't know Betty's room number, and wasn't sure he had left word with the hotel operator that he had called. The woman's English was appalling, and his Russian was worse. He had repeated, "Tell her Jon, her husband, called" again and again.

He slammed the phone down in frustration and pounded his fist on the table.

Two days had passed since Jon had determined that he had to get to Kiev. And if obstructions were indicators of the importance of his mission, his being there was very important indeed. To make matters worse, he had a full-blown cold, which was quickly settling into his chest. He was trying to accomplish everything with a 102-degree fever.

No one had been kinder to him than Joyce during the past forty-eight hours. As was her way, she felt the pain of others deeply, sometimes experiencing the heartache of others herself. This particular heartache never left her; she loved Jon and Betty and couldn't bear the thought of their drifting apart. Worst of all, Joyce had a persistent feeling that things were going to get worse before they got better. She couldn't explain it. It sounded negative and pessimistic. But there it was, a gloomy premonition that she shared with no one but God.

As for the Almighty, Jon had renewed his communication with Him rather dramatically, particularly since his isolated weeks in the Yukon. In all the difficulties he was encountering, he really had no place else to turn. Joyce was wonderfully kind, and he knew she was praying for Betty and him. Jim was generous in his efforts to help but seemed as confounded as Jon with the logistics. Most of Jon's other friends were unbelievers, and confiding in them about personal issues was unthinkable.

One day the new phone line was ringing when Jon walked in. It was Betty's father, Harold.

"How's that daughter of mine getting along overseas?" he asked.

"I wish I knew. I haven't been able to get a call through, Harold."

Jon sneezed explosively a couple of times, causing Harold to involuntarily yank the receiver away from his ear in an effort to spare what was left of his hearing.

After Jon had trumpeted into a handkerchief several times, Harold continued. "Look, son, I'm not about to turn into a meddling old man, but to tell you the truth, I've been worried about you two."

"What are you worried about, Harold?"

"Oh, you're off in the Yukon, and she's off in Russia or somewhere. She's not a bad-looking woman, and you're a red-blooded man. What's to keep either one of you from getting into trouble?"

"Harold, there's not another woman in the world for me."

"Yeah, I know. But you know what they say, 'out of sight, out of mind.'"

Jon started to defend his allegiance to Betty when he was seized by another series of sneezes. He sputtered and snorted a little before Harold continued. "I'm not saying either one of you is looking around. But don't forget, I was a Marine for a long time, and I've seen a lot of water go under the bridge. You two better find a way to stay under the same roof."

"I understand, Harold. It's just that our careers take us in different directions."

Harold paused, taking a brief moment to figure out what the world was coming to. He sighed in resignation. "Well, you hang in there, Jon. And don't get too far afield, you know what I mean? "

When it came to sensitive matters, the best Harold Fuller could offer was a potpourri of timeworn clichés. But, would-be pundit or not, he had an immense, caring heart. Jon smiled affectionately at his father-in-law's clumsy words. "I'd appreciate your praying for us, Harold."

"What makes you think I don't?"

Two other people had also joined the ranks of the intercessors. Jon had never met the good Doctor Dunn and his wife, and they had only heard his name in passing. But they had arrived home burdened with concern after spending the day with his wife. "I don't know what it is, Steven, but I feel almost afraid for Betty."

Steven, a man of few words, only nodded. But he took his wife's hand in his, and they sent their suspicions heavenward, amidst pleas for protection and prayers for intervention.

With all this going on around her, Betty, whose emotional extravagance was about to reap what it had already sown, awakened after a few minutes of blissful sleep. The phone in her room was ringing. She clicked on a light and glanced at her watch. It was 11:45.

"Hello?"

"Betty, did I wake you? It's Mike."

She was pleased, but puzzled.

"It's okay. Is everything all right, Mike?"

"Betty, I can't get you off my mind. Are you feeling the same things I'm feeling?"

Betty was trying to summon her faculties. "Of course, Mike. It was wonderful to see you."

"Betty, I'm . . . this is a feeling I've never had before. Would you mind if we talked a few minutes?"

"No, not at all. Go ahead."

"No, not on the phone. Can I come up to your room for a little while? I won't stay long."

It wasn't morality or propriety that made her say no initially, although both issues occurred to her after she'd hung up. It was a more practical matter: She'd washed away all her makeup, her hair was in a ponytail, and she was wearing a sweatshirt and shorts. Mike wouldn't find her nearly as attractive if he saw her like this.

"Mike, I'm already in bed. Can we talk tomorrow?"

His voice was a hoarse whisper. "I don't know if I can wait till tomorrow. Please, Betty."

She laughed nervously. "You can wait. You haven't seen me in more than a year. You can wait a few hours. I'll be gone most of the day, so call me after four."

"Betty . . ."

"Good night, Mike," she laughed again. After the receiver was back in its cradle, she stared at it for a minute. What did Mike want to talk about? Why did he want to come to her room at this hour?

She was flattered, but vaguely troubled. Mike had very clearly said that he didn't want to get in the way of her marriage to Jon. Surely that would preclude any sexual moves on his part, wouldn't it? So something else must have been on his mind. But what? What could he have meant? His voice had sounded almost desperate.

Betty snuggled back into her bed, trying to recapture her earlier euphoria. Before long she was feeling drowsy. Afraid the phone would ring again, she couldn't quite drift away. Muddled thoughts began to come and go, half-dreams and drifts of truth. Some long-forgotten Bible verse intruded on her reverie. She tried to ignore it, but it kept recurring.

"In your anger do not sin": Do not let the sun go down while you're still angry, and do not give the devil a foothold.

After that little edict had made the mental rounds a few times, Betty was wide awake, sitting up in bed, wondering why on earth that particular verse was orbiting in her head. *Why do these things always have to come back to me in the King James Version?*

She tried to connect the verse with her circumstances, but at least for the moment, she was too tired to make sense of it. Anger. Sin. Mike. What did they have to do with each other?

"Lord, if you're trying to tell me something, I'm not getting it," she informed the Creator before making a concerted effort to go back to sleep. Then, with a sudden chill, she added, ". . . I don't know what that stuff about the devil means, but I don't want him messing with me, so protect me from him, Lord."

Half a world away, Jon was answering the phone again.

"Mr. Surrey-Dixon? Ed Kramer here, in Vancouver."

"Yes, Mr. Kramer. I'm glad you called. I've been trying to get in touch with Betty, and I can't seem to get the right room number."

"I don't know the room number either, but maybe I can get it for you from the Dunns. I've been trying to get through to them for two days, but the circuits are always busy. In any case, you probably remember that Keith, my son-in-law, was going to take the photographs for the Kiev book."

"Yes. I remember."

"Well, he and my daughter are expecting a baby, and there are some complications with her pregnancy. The doctor has sent her to bed for the duration, and Keith just doesn't feel right about leaving her. I was wondering if I could hire you to do the book? I know it's rather late notice . . ."

Jon was stunned. It wasn't particularly flattering to play second-string to a Minolta autofocus, but it meant his way to Kiev would be paid. And, for that matter, maybe he would be able to get his visa a little more quickly. Kramer surely had connections with the embassies.

"I've got some free time at the moment. I'm assuming you want me to get over there right away, don't you?"

"Betty's got another two weeks there, and from what I could gather a few days ago, she's putting her material together right now. I'd like to fly you over in about a week and a half. That'll give me a little extra time to take care of the finances. I've got a few details to work out at this end."

Stung with disappointment, Jon tried to counter the offer. "Is there any way I could get to Kiev a little faster?"

Kramer was not only eccentric, he was also unable to relate to any form of spontaneity. "Faster? Why would you want to do that? I seriously doubt it. But go ahead and take care of the visas and tickets on your end, and I'll reimburse you later. I'm rather busy at the moment, so maybe you can get things organized a little more quickly. It's a slow process, you know, but maybe it'll go faster than I expect."

After agreeing upon a rather mediocre fee for his services, Jon hung up, feeling like the recipient of a good-news-bad-news message. The good news was that his way would be paid to Kiev. The bad news was that he was now in the employment of Ed Kramer, and he would have to work on something besides his marriage once he arrived in Kiev.

Jim, however, was ecstatic when he heard the news. "I've had nothing but trouble trying to get you a visa. Maybe the Lord wanted you to wait, so you wouldn't have to pay your own way."

After a couple more conversations that same day, Jon was assured that Kramer was perfectly serious about his offer. With that, he threw himself into preparations for a photography assignment and not simply for a husband's reconciliatory journey. In his spirit, he had the feeling that God was at work in the situation, bringing all the elements together in their proper order. However, in his mind, he was frustrated beyond words with all the delays. Would he ever get to Kiev?

It occurred to him that perhaps God had preparatory work to do in Betty's heart before his arrival. Maybe He wanted to soften her a bit. Or to remind her of their happiest times. Or to assure her of her husband's love.

"Lord, Your will be done," he prayed hopefully and repeatedly, fighting fear and impatience with every spiritual weapon he could muster.

When Betty's alarm went off the next morning, she was almost too exhausted to get out of bed. A combination of jet lag, her unexpected encounter with Mike, and his late-night phone call had taken their toll on her body. She lavishly smeared under-eye cream beneath her lower lids, piled on extra blush, and layered her eyelashes with mascara, all in an effort to counteract the unattractive effects of her heavy fatigue.

When she handed her room key to the hotel attendant, the heavyset young girl announced, "One moment please." There was a handwritten message in the wooden box, which she handed to Betty.

"John husband called."

Betty read the words in amazement. So that's why the message light had been on when she got back to the room. *Just in time to make me feel guilty,* she smirked. Nevertheless, hope flickered faintly somewhere inside her. Jon had tried to reach her. At first she was disappointed that she'd missed the call. Then she remembered the poem. He'd read the poem, and it had worried him. He'd tried to call, no doubt in response to its rather final tone. *Good. Maybe he needs to squirm a little.*

With the note still in her hand, she slid into the Dunns' back seat. On the way to the hospital, she yawned several times.

"Betty, you're tired, aren't you? We could have let you sleep in if we'd known." Marian turned with sincere concern on her face.

She's a nice woman.

"It's just jet lag. I'm fine."

"Any word from home? Has your husband been able to get through?"

Betty smiled and showed her the note still folded in her hand. "He called last night while I was . . . at dinner."

"It's a shame you missed his call. It's so hard to get through from the States. I'll bet you've been homesick, haven't you?"

"Oh, not really. We're both pretty much used to traveling."

"But if you've only been married a year, I'm sure you miss each other when you're apart."

Betty could almost feel Mike Brody's physical presence as they talked about Jon. He was kissing her hair.

He was squeezing her hand. He was holding her tightly on the dance floor. The memory of his advances made her feel uncomfortable.

"Oh, yes, I think about Jon. But I can't let myself get all upset about missing him when I'm supposed to be working."

"What's he like, Betty?"

"Jon?"

"Yes."

"Well, as you know, he's a photographer. He's tall and thin, kind of red-headed with blue eyes. He's from New Zealand, so he has a bit of an accent. We like a lot of the same things, you know, poetry and music and traveling and world affairs . . ." Betty's voice trailed off, and in her weariness she felt tears collecting somewhere behind her eyes.

Oh, God. Why does it have to be like this?

"You two sound like a wonderful match. I wish we could meet him. You know, Steven and I were always interested in the same things, too. We weren't just attracted to each other romantically, although that was always part of our chemistry. But we genuinely loved talking to each other and learning from each other. It was such fun, because our interests were the same, yet each of us specialized in something the other needed to know." Marian's voice was vibrant with enthusiasm. "It may sound a little corny, but our marriage really has gotten to be a never-ending discovery."

"I could see that in the two of you the minute I met you," Betty nodded. "I have to admit, it's pretty unusual to see that kind of friendship between two married people. Most couples barely speak."

Steven chuckled. "Marian and I don't talk all the time, but then we don't have to."

"What he means to say is, *he* doesn't talk all the time because *I* do!" Marian said, throwing her head back and laughing.

"Jon and I used to be more that way than we are right now," Betty volunteered, immediately wishing she hadn't.

"Any particular reason?"

"Oh, I guess life got in the way."

"Well, just between us, we had our problems at the beginning, too, Betty. Someday I'll tell you about it."

"I can't imagine you and Steven having problems, Marian."

"We'd filed for divorce twice before we'd been married two years."

"What happened?"

"We were going in separate directions, and we both got infatuated with other people. It's kind of a long story. I'll tell you about it some other time. Right now, we'd better get inside."

They had parked in front of the hospital and were getting out of the car when Betty noticed someone moving quickly out of sight along the side of the building. It was a quiet, secluded facility, and the movement seemed incongruous with the surroundings.

They went inside, and Betty began to interview the first child. Marian translated and helped her word the questions sensitively. Steven was making his rounds. After a fairly comprehensive chat with the first child, Marian lifted the youngster into a wheelchair and left to return her to her room.

She hadn't been out of the room long when Mike Brody appeared in the doorway. Betty was more frightened than pleased.

"Mike? What are you doing here? "

"I had to see you." His eyes were strangely intense, and his face was pale. "I had to see you again."

Betty stared at him silently.

"Can we go to the club again tonight?"

Even if she'd wanted to say no, Betty was quite sure she should say yes, if for no other reason than to prevent an unpleasant scene in the clinic.

"Of course. I'll meet you there at seven,"

He started to moved toward her, to reach for her, when Marian returned, pushing a tiny, bald-headed boy in the wheelchair.

"Oh, excuse me," he said instantly and almost miraculously composing himself. "I'm Mike—a friend of Betty's. I was driving by when I saw her get out of the car. Just came in to say hi. See you later, Betty."

He waved as he left, his grin affable and his manner self-assured.

Betty's hands were shaking. She hoped Marian wouldn't notice, knowing very well that she would. She took a deep breath. Once Mike was out of earshot, she commented, "Well, *that* was a surprise."

"I didn't know you had friends here in Kiev." Marian's eyes were fixed on Betty's tense face.

"I didn't know he was here, either. I ran into him in the hotel last night."

"Is he a good friend?"

"Not really," she said, shivering unexpectedly. "I've met him a couple of times before. But to tell you the truth, I really don't know him very well at all."

7

Of all the Chernobyl children Betty interviewed, Dmitry was her favorite. He was deteriorating rapidly, and Steven didn't expect him to live more than a few weeks. But his sweet, affectionate personality touched Betty. He had a crooked smile and a quick wit, and he was unusually astute for a child of nine.

Marian had wheeled him into the office just in time to interrupt Mike Brody's visit. He had watched the proceedings with interest and said something to Marian, which she translated for Betty.

"Was that your boyfriend?"

Betty's heart pounded, but she smiled at the boy fondly. "No, Dmitry, he's a friend. I'm married, you know."

"I think he likes you," Dmitry added, and Marian translated.

Betty and Marian's eyes met. "Friends always like each other," she countered gently. "Besides, Dmitry, I think we're here to talk about you, not me."

Dmitry's green eyes glittered with life, contradicting the withering condition of his body. His skin had a yellowish cast, and his hair had long ago fallen out, leaving him with an extraterrestrial look. Of all the children, he was the only one who spoke of heaven. In his child's way, he was looking forward to a better world: strong legs, a full head of flaxen hair, and no more hospitals.

Betty's eyes teared more than once while she talked to him. How could someone so full of life be so close to death? His dream of eternity troubled her. She was doing her best to avoid spiritual concerns, but with little success. This little boy had nothing else to hope for. She stifled an impulse to ask him to pray for her when they were saying good-bye.

It was about four in the afternoon when Betty and the Dunns made their way back to the hotel. As they drove, Marian turned around and said, "Betty, why don't you come to dinner at our flat tonight? We'd love to have you."

"I can't, Marian. I told Mike, the man you met today in the office, that I'd have dinner with him."

"Does he know Jon?" Marian inquired tactfully.

"Oh, yes, he and Jon were together in Wiesbaden after Jon's release. He was part of Jon's debriefing team."

"Well, we'd love to have you come some other night. Maybe tomorrow?"

"Of course. I'd really like to spend some time with you two."

When Betty got out of the car, she gave Marian a hug. "Don't worry about me, now. I'm fine."

"I wouldn't want to be a woman alone at the Hotel Rus. Or anywhere else, for that matter."

Betty made her way to her room and stretched out on the bed, feeling rather exhausted. She hadn't been there five minutes when the phone rang. "Hi! It's Mike. Why don't you meet me, and we'll go for a walk?"

"Where are you?"

"I'm downstairs. Come on down."

"I will, but give me a few minutes. I want to change clothes . . ." *and rest,* she added silently. Again she stretched out. *Just a little rest . . .*

Five minutes later, another ring of the phone jarred her.

"Betty, I thought you were coming down."

An unexpected annoyance rose in her. She was flattered, yes. But Mike was being a little too pushy.

"I'm not quite ready," she responded brightly. "I want to change."

Stretching and yawning, she pulled a blue chambray dress over her head and exchanged her tan shoes for navy ones. As she brushed out her long, blonde hair she could see that the purple circles under her eyes were no less evident than they'd been that morning. Afraid Mike would call again, she quickly smeared some cover-up over them, freshened her lipstick, and headed for the elevator.

Despite his initial aggressiveness, Mike couldn't have been more delightful that afternoon. They walked down a hill on the backside of the hotel and found themselves in a quiet, older neighborhood where women pushed babies in old-fashioned prams and children in brightly colored clothes played ball in courtyards. The city's buildings, once elegant, were in sad need of repair. Still, they bore a certain dignity. And a wealth of chestnut trees, crowned in their finest summer greenery, dappled every boulevard and lane with ever-changing displays of light and shadow.

Twice, as they attempted to cross busy intersections, Mike took Betty's hand. But he did so protectively and released it once they'd stepped back onto the sidewalk. Betty thought about Jon more than once. They were surrounded by such lovely scenes, and she imagined him taking spectacular photographs. She missed him. And, either in spite of or because of Mike's company, she kept wondering how he was.

Maybe her anger was gradually dissipating. Or maybe subconsciously she had deemed Mike's company as an appropriate reprisal for Jon's crimes. In any case, Jon seemed to her a less-cavalier scoundrel that afternoon. And Mike was simply a pleasant friend whose fellowship was more than welcome.

They found themselves at an outdoor cafe on a hillside adjacent to the Dinamo Stadium. They ordered sodas and sipped them in the liquid summer sunlight. Betty felt Mike's eyes on her and enjoyed the attention, but she didn't return his gaze. She was absorbing the sights and sounds of Kiev, and reveling in its Old-World ambiance.

Making their way back into town, they located a post office where Betty purchased stamps for postcards. That night she planned to write everyone back home. Now that she thought about it, Jon's would be the first card she would send. Rather than aggravating his worry, she was ready to let him know that, although she was having a perfectly good time without him, he was on her mind.

Naturally she wouldn't mention Mike.

At the moment, Mike Brody was no cause for concern anyway. Polite and proper, he'd been on his best behavior all afternoon. There was no trace of the neediness his eyes had mirrored that morning. She smiled, suddenly remembering little Dmitry's childlike comment, "I think he likes you." What a precious child he was.

When they arrived back at the Hotel Rus, Mike kissed her on the cheek, rather softly, and whispered something unintelligible in her ear as he left her.

Forgetting her plans with the Dunns, Betty agreed to have dinner with him the following night. She wanted to spend tonight alone in her room, writing cards, sleeping, and organizing her notes. Mike seemed to have something to do himself, and she was quite happy to see him go.

Betty's room was about as unluxurious as a hotel room could be. It was worse than anything she'd ever encountered, even in the heart of East Africa. The Ugandan orphanage had been sparsely furnished, but it was one of the friendliest communities she had ever visited. Kiev was a different matter. The liveliness of Kampala was nowhere to be found. The people mostly went through the motions of living. There was no enthusiasm anywhere.

The water in the Hotel Rus bathroom was never more than tepid, and for several days it had been completely cold. When Betty inquired about it at the front desk, the attendant offered a shrug in a reply and returned unsmiling to his tasks. She thanked God several times for her hot pot, which provided enough hot water for washing her hair and sponge bathing.

Meanwhile, if the hotel had laundry facilities, the necessary arrangements for locating and using them were beyond her comprehension. According to the Dunns, the prices were astronomical. They had finally taken her laundry to a friend's washing machine. Two days later she was beginning to think that her clothes had been sold at some local black market.

Betty had lugged a laptop computer along on the journey, the use of which had proved to be a welcome diversion. No matter what else might have been on her mind, once she began to write about the children, every other concern faded into insignificance. The ailing children were so lovable and so very unhealthy. She wanted to take them all home with her, buy them big down comforters, feed them American treats, and give them the best medical care available. Some latent maternal instinct was putting out tiny shoots and entangling her soul with Chernobyl's little victims. It was a dangerous devotion, too, because not one of them was likely to live for more than a year or two.

It's not fair, Lord, she thought, staring out the window at a bank of thunder clouds. *Or maybe it is. Maybe they'll be happier in heaven than they'd ever be as adults here in Kiev.*

Adulthood had taken its toll on Betty in recent weeks. Moving across eleven time zones hadn't helped either. By seven o'clock, with curtains closed and computer clicked off, she was fast asleep.

Somewhere in the depths of a dream, she found herself in Laguna Beach, sitting at the foot of her tower. She was watching the surf and writing something on a long, blue scroll. Dressed in a flowing gown, she saw herself from a distance. Flashes of light colored the horizon, and the sound of distant thunder rumbled far away.

Apocalyptic images flashed in and out of the scene. There were violent upheavals of earth and water. She saw signs in the heavens—a cloud appeared, looking like a Lamb, and stars seemed to be falling, visible even in the daylight. Pentagrams and goats' heads appeared on people's clothing, while other men and women in white robes carried crosses in their hands and wore lilies in their hair. The world was in chaos, and yet in the midst there were intervals of great peace.

Between the nightmarish episodes, she was back at the Laguna tower, diligently recording something on her blue scroll. And Jon was always beside her; in fact she was leaning against him as she wrote.

All at once, a particularly loud clap of thunder rattled across her consciousness, awakening her. She jumped out of bed, yanked the curtain aside, and stared out the window. The Kiev sky was alive with lightning.

Betty tried to remember everything about her bizarre dream. It must have represented some sort of battle between good and evil. Clearly the elaborate ornamentations of Kiev's Eastern Orthodox churches were woven into the fabric of the vision. She couldn't quite grasp her dream's significance, although she was strangely comforted by the fact that Jon had been beside her even in the throes of the worst pandemonium.

More than anything else she wanted to recapture the words she had been writing on the blue scroll. She turned on a light and grabbed a notebook. Little by little, fragments of the message came back to her. She wrote them down and filled in the rest with her imagination.

> Where are we going?
> Who can guess?
> Beyond the horizon,
> More or less.
>
> What will we find there?
> Who can tell?
> One man's heaven
> Is another man's hell.

Strange words, strange dream. She trembled, pondering every possible meaning, listening to the rain that splattered against her window. The words that had come to her just the day before returned to her memory—"Be angry and sin not . . . do not give place to the devil." Was she involved in some sort of a spiritual battle? Again the puzzle: anger, sin, and the devil.

Searching herself for clues, only one incident came to mind. With a chill, she remembered the strange expression she'd seen in Mike Brody's eyes earlier that morning. If she hadn't known him better, she would have described it as diabolical. Quite apart from that, she was also unhappy about his sudden appearance at the children's hospital. What had possessed him to go there looking for her?

Mike was a perfect gentleman this afternoon. It was just my imagination playing tricks on me this morning.

Nevertheless, she did take a moment to pray, something she'd done infrequently of late. "Lord," she whispered, "If You're trying to tell me something, please help me understand. And keep me safe, Lord. That was a really scary dream."

Despite Ed Kramer's financial involvement in the process, Jon was having an exceptionally difficult time trying to get to Betty. Fortunately, the more challenging the arrangements proved to be, the more determined he was to overcome them. Something was prodding him. Call it fear, insecurity, or sheer tenacity, he was going to Kiev with or without a visa, with or without an airline ticket, with or without Kramer's assistance.

After several calls to the fledgling Ukrainian Embassy in Washington, Jon was able to get a promise that if he would Fed Ex his passport and a check to them, he would have his travel documents back, visa and all, the following day. Silently appealing for mercy as he handed the envelope to the Fed Ex representative, he anxiously waited for morning to call D.C. When he talked with the embassy, they confirmed that they had received his passport.

Relieved, he went about his business. The following day he stayed home, waiting for the return delivery. By one o'clock, it still hadn't arrived. He called again. "It is still on the visa officer's desk, Mr. Surrey-Dixon. She is ill today. My apologies."

"Isn't there anybody else there who can issue a visa?"

"No sir."

"How sick is she?" He tried diligently to keep his voice friendly.

"I don't know, sir. She did not say."

Three days later, the passport arrived, visa intact. Jon began to follow up on the calls he'd made about flights. The London flights were no problem, but the connections to Moscow were either booked solid or canceled. He was beginning to feel a growing desperation. Everything seemed to be against him. It was almost frightening.

Desperately, Jon called a travel-agent friend, who agreed to search for ticket consolidators. "One of these guys might very well have a block of tickets to Moscow. I'll get back to you."

Another two days passed. Jon called Ed Kramer, almost despairing. "Any suggestions?" Jon asked, hoping Kramer wouldn't insist on taking over the arrangements himself. Jon very much needed to be doing something about the trip besides waiting for a phone call from Vancouver.

"Don't worry, you'll get there. It's always like this. I had to send Betty over two days early because something opened up at the last minute."

Jon felt he needed to call Betty to let her know he was coming. But the busy circuits he'd broken through several days before were unrelenting this time. He sat by the phone for hours at a time, pushing the redial button to no avail. His emotions swung between resignation and panic, like a pendulum ticking away the wasted, empty days.

Sometimes the chilling words of Betty's poem came into his mind. "Haven't you twisted me enough?" And sometimes the verse from Jeremiah replayed in his thoughts, "I will give them singleness of heart and action . . ." The two concepts seemed diametrically opposed to each other, and the one from Betty wasn't a "Bible promise." It was a cold, hard reality, written in her own hand.

Sometimes faith requires individuals to overlook tangible reality in light of some higher, unseen truth. Such a demand, however, is rarely met without deep doubts and immense intellectual struggles.

And Jon Surrey-Dixon was struggling. He fought persistent anger and growing alarm. Night after night, he fell into bed exhausted and discouraged. About the time he went to sleep, prayers on his lips for the healing of their marriage, Betty was walking out the hotel door. She was heading for the Dunns' car, the children's hospital, and some inevitable meeting with Mike Brody.

That Friday Kiev was rain-washed and ablaze with sunlight as Betty and the Dunns made their way across puddled streets to the hospital.

"We got a call last night that Dmitry is failing," Steven reported to Betty. "He's pretty bad."

Betty, saddened by the news, asked if she could see the child. "No matter what happens, I want to feature him in the book. He's such a precious little boy."

"His mother has been with him all night, and I'm sure she wouldn't mind a visit from you. In fact, if you want, you could interview her, too."

"She's probably in no mood to talk to a nosy American at the moment."

Marian nodded. "It could be a bad time, but it also might be helpful for her to talk. Let's see how things are when we get there."

As it turned out, the atmosphere in Dmitry's room was very serious indeed. The child had endured a terrible night, and his body was limp with fever. His eyes, usually sparkling with life, were glazed and only flickered with recognition when Betty came into the drab ward he shared with several children. At his side sat a frail, waif-like woman. Sophia's thin blonde hair was wispy and uncombed, and her brown eyes stared vacantly at her son's guests.

Marian explained who Betty was in a very quiet voice. She told Sophia how much Dmitry and Betty enjoyed each other. "I think she'll cheer him up a bit," she said in Russian. The young mother smiled wearily and nodded in assent.

Betty placed her hand on Dmitry's hot forehead. "I hear you've been having a hard time," she spoke tenderly to him.

Once he understood, he nodded and murmured something, which Marian translated. "I have been thinking about heaven again," he said.

Betty nodded. "So have I. I had a dream last night that reminded me of heaven."

Dmitry's eyes widened slightly. "So did I . . ."

"What did you dream, Dmitry?"

His voice was a whisper. "I dreamed I was there and that Jesus told me I couldn't stay. He said I had to come back to my mother."

Betty, Marian, and Sophia looked at each other in surprise. "How did you feel about that, Dmitry?" Marian asked the boy.

"I was sorry in a way, because heaven was very beautiful. But He told me I had things to do here and then I could come back. So I know I'll get to go there later. Besides He doesn't want me to leave Mother alone."

Like starlight, obscured by clouds and then unveiled, hope suddenly began to flicker, ever so faintly, in Sophia's eyes. Betty surprised herself by asking, "Could we pray together for Dmitry?" She wasn't sure if she was breaking some sort of cultural taboo, but the impulse was irresistible.

Placing her palm firmly on the boy's bare, scorching head, she spoke with surprising confidence. "Lord, this is Your son, Dmitry, and he's very sick. You are the only One who can help him. And because You said You'd heal the sick if Your people would pray, the three of us are asking You, in agreement, to touch this boy and restore him to health. If You spoke to Him in a dream, Lord, we want to honor that. We're asking You to make him well so he can do the things You want him to do without suffering so much. In Jesus' name, amen."

Marian didn't interpret the prayer for reasons of her own, but her eyes were wet with tears when Betty finished praying.

Sophia said, "*Spasibo*," very softly, then repeated "thank you" in English, and squeezed Betty's hand.

Something happened in there, Betty told herself as they walked back out into the hall. *I had to pray for him. I hope I didn't offend anybody, but I had to do it, no matter what. Lord, please. Make him get better.*

The rest of the day passed without incident. Dmitry slept almost constantly, and Steven didn't disturb his sleep even to examine him. The boy appeared to have passed through the crisis, and for the moment that was good news enough.

Interviewing some of the other children, Betty added some important details to her notes. In an effort not to tire them out, she questioned them only a few minutes each day. As a result, her sense of continuity wasn't impressive. Nevertheless, she had an overall confidence that the book was as good or maybe even better than the Ugandan book had been at the same stage.

Just before they left the hospital, Marian remarked, "I hope you like the fish we're having tonight. It's a popular one out here, but some Westerners aren't too fond of it."

Betty caught her breath. She'd told Mike she'd have dinner with him that evening, and there wasn't any way to let him know she couldn't make it. Even if she went back to the hotel, there was no place to leave a message for him. She had no idea where he was staying. It was odd, she reminded herself, that he was such a secretive person.

Realizing she had no options, Betty headed home with the Dunns, determined to enjoy the evening with them. And she did.

Their tiny apartment was barely the size of Betty's living room and kitchen in Laguna Beach. Every wall was lined with books, floor to ceiling. A small stereo system was packed in between the books in the sitting area. Facing the stereo was a settee, a vintage 1950s floor lamp, and an enameled coffee table. One corner of the room held a lace-covered wooden dinette table with two ladder-back chairs, and next to that was a miniature kitchen, tidy but crammed with jars, utensils, and tinned foods. The Dunns' bedroom barely had room for a quilt-topped double bed and the ubiquitous books. Their bathroom, although equally small, did have an adequate shower, which Betty had gratefully enjoyed on the day of her arrival.

Steven brought one of the kitchen chairs into the sitting room, and the three of them dined, drank tea, and chatted the evening away to the strains of the London Symphony Orchestra. They talked about Canada and the medical profession in Russia and the Ukraine. They discussed psychology and Christianity and how the two could be mingled to the benefit of all who would examine the "hidden places" of their hearts. They considered the plight of the Chernobyl victims, the rumors that persisted about continuous radiation leaks in the area, and the distinct possibility of another similar tragedy.

Finally, before Betty's departure, Marian turned the

conversation toward her. "Tell us about your family, Betty. Are your parents in California, too?"

"No, my mother's dead, and my father's in Oregon. I'm the only child—no brothers or sisters."

"Are you close to your dad?"

"Oh, he's a funny old guy. When I was small, I was his golden girl, but the older I got the more he pulled away from me. I think he wanted to give my mother his full attention. She was his pride and joy, and I was a sickly, opinionated child who didn't always agree with their ideas. Since she died, he and I have been a little closer, especially during the hostage situation with Jon. My dad really took an interest in that."

"So I take it he approves of your husband?"

"Oh, yes. He thinks Jon's great. He just doesn't approve of my traveling, Jon's traveling, and our being apart so much."

Marian and Steven glanced at each other, as if on cue. "Considering some of the things we've been through, we'd probably hope you could spend more time together, too." Steven commented, looking at his wife as if she were the only person in the world.

Betty inhaled heavily and glanced at her watch. It was getting to be time to go back to the hotel. In conclusion Betty offered an amazing understatement. "It's something Jon and I probably need to talk about when I get back."

Marian wasn't quite finished with her investigation. "How well do you communicate with Jon? Do you feel pretty free to say whatever you want?"

Betty considered the question carefully. "Only when I'm mad," she laughed. "No, I suppose I could be more direct. He probably wouldn't mind, but I hate arguments, so I guess I keep things to myself when I shouldn't."

"Did your parents get angry when you expressed your feelings to them?"

"Well, I guess I got put in my place a few times. My parents didn't believe children had a right to any feelings unless they were in total agreement with theirs. I think that's one of the things that caused my father to lose interest in me. I disagreed with him and Mother too often when I was a teenager."

"If your father withdrew his attention from you as you grew up, you may be expecting the same thing to happen with Jon. We girls have to be careful not to let history repeat itself."

Betty made an effort not to roll her eyes heavenward. *Here we go with the inner-child-of-the-past stuff.* Summoning an appropriate psychological term from her mental thesaurus, Betty inquired, "Are you talking about self-fulfilling prophecy or something like that?"

Marian smiled kindly. "Well, suppose you always felt that your mother was coming between you and your father. The chances are you're going to be very sensitive if Jon pays any attention to another woman."

Somewhere inside Betty's right brain, a name appeared in a blaze of lights.

CARLA.

Carla. Perfect. So you're saying I'm turning Carla into a latter-day version of my mother because Jon's paying attention to her? Oh, please. Give me a break!

"That's an interesting idea, Marian." Betty casually rechecked her watch. "You know, I hate to say this, but I've got to get back to the hotel and do some work before I fall asleep. I'm trying to type up our interviews every night so I don't have to do it all at once."

Marian, aware that she and her suggestions had been at least temporarily dismissed, stood up. Her voice was warm as ever. "By the way, Betty, I forgot to tell you, but we have your laundry hanging in our bedroom closet. Steven, why don't you get it for her?"

Betty reached for her purse, more than happy to pay them for the laundry services.

"No, you don't! It's our pleasure," Marian beamed, hugging Betty graciously. "I'll let Steven drive you home while I take a nice hot shower. See you tomorrow, Betty. It's been great talking to you."

At the Hotel Rus, Steven walked Betty as far as the elevators. He failed to see the dark-haired man standing impatiently in the lobby bar, watching them bid each other good night. "Don't work too hard, Betty." Steven smiled cheerily and waved good-bye.

Striding past as quickly as possible without running, Betty scrupulously ignored the eighth-floor lounge lizards, every one clad in their striped pajamas, absorbed in the green-hued television screen. She unlocked her room and was not surprised to see the message light on. She called the front desk. The night clerk informed her in rather fractured English, "Three calls from Mr. Mike, yes?"

"What do they say?"

"He call later."

She hung up, sincerely wishing she hadn't forgotten to tell Mike about her plans with the Dunns. She hoped his feelings hadn't somehow been hurt. Three messages? Well, maybe he was moving around town and just checked from time to time to see if she was in.

Just then the phone rang. "Betty?" The voice was brittle. "Thanks a million for standing me up."

"Oh, Mike, I'm really sorry. When we talked yesterday, I'd forgotten all about my dinner with the Dunns. I would have called you, but you didn't give me a number."

"How could you do this to me?"

"Mike, I'm sorry. I really am."

"I'm downstairs. Why don't you come down. I want to talk to you."

Betty had little desire to see Mike that night, but she wanted to make things right with him, so she agreed. She nervously brushed her hair, locked the door, and headed downstairs.

He was standing outside the elevator when the doors opened. His eyes were dark and brooding, and he had a drink in his hand. Without a word, he grabbed her right arm firmly below the shoulder and ushered her toward two lobby chairs.

"What are you trying to do?" he demanded.

"Mike, I don't know what you're talking about. I already explained that I was with friends and I had no way of calling you."

"Why didn't you cancel your dinner with them? You could have told them you had other plans."

Betty was beginning to feel more angry than sorry. "Because I wanted to visit with them."

"You're with them every day."

"Yes, and I've seen you every day, too. Besides, they know I'm married, and I'm not especially anxious to tell them you and I are having dinner every night."

"So you're ashamed of me?"

"That's not what I said." Her voice was even, but resolute. She didn't like the conversation, and she liked the malicious glint in his eyes even less. It suddenly occurred to her how little she knew about him and how very foolish she'd been to flirt with such a rootless character.

"Mike, I'm not going to sit here and argue with you. I've apologized, very sincerely, for what happened tonight. And I'll be glad to have dinner with you tomorrow night if you want. But that's all I can do."

With that, Mike seemed to soften a little. "You don't know how long I've been sitting here," he explained plaintively. "I've been here since 5:30 waiting for you."

She looked at him in disbelief. "Why didn't you leave?"

"Because I wanted you." His voice was very low and sounded almost rasping. "Because I wanted you."

Betty fought off the chills that were attacking the back of her neck. *There's something wrong with him.* She stood up, brushed her skirt nervously, and smiled at Mike as innocuously as possible. "I hope you had dinner, Mike."

He shook his head. "How could I eat?"

"Why don't you go get something now?"

"Will you come with me?"

Betty hesitated. "Why don't you grab something at your hotel. I'm really tired, and I've still got some work to do."

"Can I bring something up to your room and eat it there?"

"No, Mike. I don't want you in my room." *That was the wrong thing to say, Betty dear. Try again.* "I've got work to do, and I know I'd be distracted . . ."

His posture stiffened, and his face looked somber. "I'll see you at six tomorrow. If you happen to remember."

"Mike, I'm sorry. I really am. Of course I'll remember."

He sighed and attempted a pitiful smile. "Don't worry. I understand. I just want to be with you so much, Betty. You're the most beautiful woman I've ever seen."

With that, he kissed her softly on the forehead, turned, and went out the door.

Solemnly riding back up the elevator, Betty tried to comprehend whatever it was that had just happened. Mike's only attachment to her seemed to be based on the fact that he thought she was beautiful. He had never really talked to her about anything significant—except during the hostage days when they exchanged information. If possible, she knew even less about him than he did about her.

Sex! she suddenly announced to herself, as if the recipient of an unexpected mental telegram. *Sex! Don't be so naive. It's just sex. And he thought you wanted it too. How can you be so dumb when you're so smart?* She shook her head in self-recrimination.

Just as she unlocked her room, the phone rang. "Hello?"

There was a prolonged silence. She listened for overseas beeps and thought she could hear someone breathing. "Hello?" she said again.

No response.

She hung up.

Two minutes later, the same thing happened. Three times. Four times. *This is starting to remind me of Carla's game. Only this is worse.* On the fifth ring, she answered, "Yes?" as coldly as possible.

"Betty?"

"Marian?"

"Yes, it's me. Are you all right, dear?"

"I'm sorry. Someone keeps calling and hanging up. Must be a wrong number," she added. It was true. As far as she was concerned, her number *was* the wrong number.

"Why don't you take the phone off the hook?"

"What if Jon calls?"

"The odds are he'll never get through anyway. But listen, I've got some interesting news. You remember how you prayed for little Dmitry this morning?"

"Of course. How is he?"

"Well, Steven drove over there a little while ago to check on him, in case he looked like he was headed for another terrible night. Betty, he's so much better! Steven can't believe it."

Betty sat down and closed her eyes. Tears squeezed out of them anyway. "That's so wonderful, Marian. What does Steven mean by 'better'?"

"Steven said that Dmitry was sitting up in bed when he got there. His fever was gone, and he was eating. The nurse said it was the third time he'd asked for food in three hours. But the real clincher came when he got out of bed and walked across the room. He hasn't walked in months, Betty."

Betty shivered, shook her head in wonder, and then cautiously ventured into Marian's turf. "I'm sure you've thought of it, but do you think it's an emotional response to his dream about heaven?"

Marian laughed. "Betty, that boy couldn't have walked yesterday no matter how inspired he'd felt. He's practically dead. Or at least he *was*. No, I don't think we can blame this one on psychology. This is something different. Anyway, I just wanted to let you know."

"I'm so glad you called, Marian. That gives a new meaning to the whole trip here."

"Well, don't forget, you had the courage to pray. I didn't. I think maybe the Lord rewarded your faith. Have a good sleep, dear, and take that phone off the hook. It's probably some drunk and he'll keep trying unless you stop him."

You got that right, Marian.

"That's exactly what I'm going to do. See you in the morning!"

She hung up the phone and then took the receiver off the cradle. Unlike the high-tech phone lines in California with their off-the-hook warning tones, this one submitted to its unanchored position with nary a beep.

Betty was blissfully relieved by the silence and quite exhausted after an emotionally charged evening. Without even washing her face, she scooted into bed. *Thanks, Lord, for helping Dmitry,* she silently prayed. *And please help me with this Mike thing. I'm sorry if I led him on. I didn't mean to.*

Having thus cleansed her soul, she promptly fell asleep. At the same moment, Jon, who had been dialing nonstop for two solid hours, finally got past the busy circuits. Instead of dialing Betty's private number, he had decided to try the main hotel number. To his amazement, it rang.

"Mrs. Betty Surrey-Dixon, please," he enunciated as clearly as possible.

"Yes. Room 824 . . . Sorry, sir, that line is ringing busy. Please try again later."

Before he could ask to leave a message, the clerk unplugged the line. "Oh, God!" he shouted, pounding his fist into the desk. "Why can't I get through to her? The same thing happened when I tried to call from Anchorage! Busy, busy, busy! What's going on here?"

8

Little Dmitry was a different boy when Betty went to see him the next morning. Although he got very dizzy when he first stood up and didn't have strength for more than a few steps, he was determined to walk for her.

"You prayed for me! Now see what I can do?"

His mother Sophia's face looked ten years younger. Naturally, no one could say how permanent her son's improvement might be. Everybody knew that remission was not the same as healing, and only time would tell. But the woman was wonderfully relieved and had even ventured a few tentative words to Dr. Dunn about taking Dmitry home for an overnight visit if he continued to do so well.

Dmitry was Sophia's only child, and her husband had died of cancer two years before. Her loneliness since the child's hospitalization had been unspeakable. And the dream of waking up with her son beside her was almost too precious to speak aloud.

Betty watched each participant in the little drama and observed how the light of joy reflected from one face to the next. It was sobering to consider how easily that particular gathering might have been at a deathbed rather than in the celebration of a healing had God not intervened.

She recalled the early days of her own reprieve from the excema that had so marred her childhood. Every morning for weeks, she had nervously tossed aside her blankets and headed straight for the bathroom mirror where she'd searched for new evidence. Was the disease really gone or not? What would trigger a relapse? Was there any sign of one?

Dreams of infirmity had haunted those first nights of health. And in her wakeful hours, the fear of the affliction's returning was unrelenting. Once she had experienced normal life, it seemed unbearable to readjust to a ceaseless battle with itching and stinging and bleeding and ugliness.

Hope is a dangerous emotion, she concluded privately.

With a last quick squeeze of Dmitry's hand, she excused herself and retreated to the office. There she prepared herself for several hours of interviews with other children. There would be time with Marta, a red-haired menace, who was a Chernobyl orphan and the last survivor in her family. And there was Gurgin, a somber five-year-old with an improved prognosis, thanks to Dr. Dunn's research. And Tanya, a bespectacled reader and lover of the poet Pushkin, who reminded Betty of herself at twelve years old.

She organized her notes, praying now and then for Dmitry and believing that he would somehow be all right. Marian came in after a few minutes, bringing along a cup of tea for Betty. "That's quite a picture, isn't it?" she remarked, referring to Dmitry.

Before Betty could answer, Mike Brody stepped into the doorway and stood watching the two women without a word. His expression was enigmatic; his tall, muscular form seemed menacing.

"Hello, Betty," he said quietly.

"Mike! What are you doing here?" she responded, far too brightly. *You're nuts, aren't you?*

"I was driving by and thought I'd come in and say hello."

"Well, hello. Marian, I think you've met Mike Brody?"

"Hi, Mike. Can I get you a cup of tea?"

"No, no thanks. I'm on my way back to town. I was just stopping by to remind you that we're having dinner tonight, Betty."

"I hadn't forgotten."

"Good. Well, I'll see you at the hotel at six, Betty. Have a good day."

With a polite nod to Marian, he walked out the door. Betty glanced out the window and saw him get into a new-looking black coupe, which he quickly drove away.

Marian was staring at her, and she could well imagine why. "I'm starting to feel a little uncomfortable about him," Betty volunteered.

"Did you invite him to come by here? I mean it's fine if you did, but . . ."

"Of course not. I don't want him coming by here. For some reason he . . . I think he scares me a little bit, Marian. One minute he's nice and the next he's possessive, as if he owned me."

"You did say that he knows you're married, didn't you?"

"Yes, he was part of Jon's debriefing team."

"He's some sort of an intelligence agent or something?"

"Something like that. To tell you the truth, I don't know much about him, except that he keeps showing up and wanting to see me. I don't see how he could be doing much work, he spends so much time hanging around. Maybe he's just lonely, but it kind of bothers me in a way."

"What would your husband say if he knew?"

Betty softly blew a puff of breath through her lips and shook her head. "He wouldn't like it. I don't think he would have objected to my having dinner with Mike once, but he wouldn't like this stuff."

"Maybe you ought to tell Mike you don't want to see him again."

"I'm going to, tonight at dinner. I've had enough of this."

"Do you think you should even have dinner with him?"

"There's no way for me to call him and cancel—I don't have a phone number. It's okay, Marian."

"You call us if you have any trouble. That hotel isn't a very safe place, if you ask me."

Betty was telling the truth, although she wasn't telling the whole truth and nothing but the truth. She wasn't about to inform Marian about her experience with Mike at Wiesbaden, or about her flirtation with Jerry Baldwin during her first marriage. She knew very well that her behavior with Mike Brody had been inappropriate, no matter how disillusioned she'd been with Jon. She was ashamed of herself and more than ready to get rid of Mike, once and for all.

"Uh, Marian?" she said, after a few minutes of silence. "Could I ask you and Steven one small favor?"

"Of course, Betty. What is it?"

"If you ever meet my husband—and you probably never will, but if you do—please don't say anything about Mike to him. I've got some other things to work out with Jon, and this mess would just make matters worse."

Marian nodded. "I don't know when we'd have the opportunity to talk about it, but you can be sure we won't. I just hope you don't run into trouble with Mike when you tell him good-bye. He seems unusually, uh, . . . persistent."

"Well, you know people better than I do, but I think if I just explain my feelings, it'll be fine."

"I hope so. But like I said, call us, night or day, if you need us."

She thinks I'm a tramp, Betty informed herself. *She thinks she's caught me in the middle of an affair and that I'm covering up. Oh, God! How do I get into these things?*

Once the day's work was completed to everyone's satisfaction, Betty popped into Dmitry's room to say good-bye.

"Thank you for praying for me," he smiled at Betty.

"You pray for me, too, Dmitry," she replied with a grin. *From the look of things, I need it worse than you do.*

Dreading the evening, she bade farewell to the Dunns, giving Marian a rather helpless smile. "Don't forget what I told you," Marian encouraged her. "We're just a phone call away."

Betty returned to her room, trying to rehearse the lines that would erase Mike Brody from the picture once and for all.

She considered the flattering approach. "You're so attractive, I can hardly resist you, and I've got to stop tempting myself like this. I'm married, and I don't want to be unfaithful to my husband."

She tried on an abrupt style. "Look, I don't appreciate your acting like you own me. Just get lost and stay lost. I don't ever want to hear from you or see you again."

She practiced an emotional, fragile speech. "Oh, Mike. I'm just so confused. Life has been difficult, and you've brought such pleasure to my otherwise bleak existence. However . . ."

"Oh, shut up, Betty!" she finally commanded herself. "Why don't you just go down there, have dinner, and say what you have to say when the time comes?" With that, she briefly primped and preened, not wanting to look too good, and headed for the elevator, breathing only one prayer as she went. "God, help me . . ."

Mike took her in his arms the moment he saw her and warmly kissed the top of her head. "Beautiful. You are the most beautiful woman I've ever known, Betty."

His seductive spell had been permanently broken, and Betty was as alert as a wartime sentry. She braced herself and decided to be flippant. "I'll bet you say that to all the girls."

"Betty, I'm not just saying that. Look at you." He held her at arm's length and surveyed her. "Beautiful face, beautiful body . . ."

Although she wasn't a completely naive woman, Betty had more than once in her life confused innocent flirtation with outright sexuality. Even Mike's seductive call a few nights before hadn't registered in her mind as a clear-cut proposition; she'd honestly believed at the time that he'd wanted to talk to her. But now her eyes were open and fear rippled inside her. *Beautiful body? Why are you looking at my body?*

They went up the mezzanine stairs to the Red Room, where they'd been before. They were seated at a smaller table this time, and Mike pulled his chair very close to Betty's.

"Did you have a good day?" he asked, placing his left palm near her right knee. He stroked her thigh a couple of times.

"Mike . . ." he gave her a puzzled look as she lifted his

hand from her leg. Impulsively he squeezed her fingers. "Mike, I'm married!"

Her fear returned, this time mingled with guilt. She glanced around the room. Had anyone been watching? There wasn't a soul there that she knew, but she scooted her chair away from Mike's ever so slightly, hoping he wouldn't notice.

He did. "Betty, if you knew how wonderful it is for me to be with you, you wouldn't be so prim and proper. I travel alone so much of the time; just being here with you is heaven on earth." His voice lowered to a husky tone. "I can't get enough of you."

"You'll have had enough of me by the time I go home, Mike. I'm not only prim and proper, I'm an absolute prude. In fact, I think this is going to be our last dinner together."

Another man's ardor might have been cooled by Betty's words. But Mike was stimulated. He loved a challenge, and he possessed supreme confidence in his sexual prowess. It had rarely failed him, even in far less ideal circumstances.

"Betty, I respect you and your values more than you know. One of the things I like about you is your strong character. I've always admired that." At that point their food arrived, and the flattering onslaught abated while Mike satisfied a less inappropriate hunger. Betty, in the meantime, pushed her food around her plate, barely able to swallow anything.

Once they'd finished the meal, he asked her to dance again. "Just this once—you're such a great dancer. I know Jon wouldn't mind."

"I don't want to dance, Mike."

"Betty, don't take everything so seriously," Mike disarmed her with a laugh. "A dance is just a dance."

Still trying to keep things on an even keel, she relented.

Two nights before, Betty had been completely captivated by Mike's attention. How could it have seemed so innocent and friendly? Now all she felt was a deep discomfort. No amount of anger with Jon could justify this kind of infidelity.

Feeling Mike's warm breath against her neck, she pulled away, stiffening with distaste. For some reason she began to think about Mike's two visits to the hospital. She recalled the movement she'd seen near the hospital door just minutes before Mike had appeared the first time. Had he lied, saying he'd seen her as he drove by? Had he been waiting for her all along?

He was an intelligence officer, and it wouldn't have been difficult for him to determine where she was going and when—she'd followed the same schedule with the Dunns every morning. They picked her up at the hotel at 10:00 and arrived at the same hospital at 10:30. For that matter, he might well have seen her name on some passport list and could have planted himself in her path, knowing she was traveling to Kiev.

Something else bothered her even more. Looking at him now, there was no trace of the strange glint that she'd seen in his eyes—that desperate, craving look. Tonight he was warmly attentive, but he didn't seem driven, at least not overtly so. She shivered.

Enough of this.

"Mike, I'm still fighting jet lag, and I've got to get to bed. Could I excuse myself?"

He pulled her closer, and there was an unwelcome intimacy in his embrace. "Why don't you come home with me, Betty?"

"Mike, stop it!" she tried to laugh off his offer.

He laughed too, but without humor. One hand was

moving up and down her back. "Let's just finish this dance, and I'll make sure you get back to your room safely."

By now Betty was alarmed. The dance was over, and Mike was staring at her strangely. Had he been drinking before their meeting? The look was there again. He was obsessed with her—his eyes, his hands, his words. And he was completely focused on having his way.

"You don't need to walk me to my room, Mike."

"I wouldn't think of letting you go alone."

"You did before . . ."

"I know, but I was so overcome with you, I had to get away."

You think you're less overcome now? You can't keep your hands off me!

She made her voice as firm as possible. "Mike, I'd better go. I enjoy your company, but I'm married, and I don't want to get into trouble. I don't think we should see each other any more after this."

"Betty, the last thing I want to do is get either one of us in trouble. I just want to make sure you get to your room safely."

Her voice was firm and cold. "I'll get there just fine. Let's just say good-bye. It's been fun seeing you, but I don't feel right about all these dinners and dates."

By now they had reached the lobby, and she quickly jumped inside one of the elevators before he could follow. He winked at her, blew a kiss, and said, "I'm going to see you once more before I leave town."

"No, Mike," she said, but the closing doors muffled her words. Out of his clutches, she heaved a sigh of relief and leaned against the wall. Once she was in her room, she went directly to the telephone directory and focused her mind on the numbers Steven had marked. She didn't anticipate needing help or confronting an emergency, but she ought to know what to do—just in case.

Satisfied that she could reach the front desk, where someone always spoke a little English, she took a tepid shower, pulled on her sweatshirt and shorts, and slid between the starched white sheets. The phone rang.

"Betty, it's Mike. I just wanted to say good night."

"Thanks, Mike." Her words were slightly clipped. "You have a good night too."

"Betty, could I bring you something to help you sleep? An after-dinner drink? Or some tea?"

"Mike, I'm already in bed, and I'm not going to have a bit of trouble going to sleep . . . *unless the phone rings again.* Thanks anyway. Bye."

She clicked the line with her finger and considered taking it off the hook. *But what if Jon calls?* Jon . . .

Tears came into her eyes, and in her exhaustion she was unable to resist them. She began to cry. How could she have allowed things to go this far with Mike? She should never have allowed him to become so affectionate. Affectionate, nothing. He was trying to get her into bed—and had been all along. It wasn't right, and she recognized it all too well, all too late.

"Lord, I'm sorry. I was so mad at Jon that I couldn't see what I was doing. This is getting out of hand, though, and I need Your help . . ."

There was a knock at the door. She stiffened in fear. "Who is it?"

"Betty? It's me. I brought you a drink."

"I don't want a drink!" she snapped. "Mike, I need to sleep. Please go away. I'll talk to you tomorrow or the next day."

"Betty, let me in." Although she couldn't see his face,

she knew that desperate look was in his eyes. It terrified her. There was something insane about all this.

"No! Mike, you've got to go. Please leave me alone!"

"I want to talk to you." The door rattled as he shook it from the outside. What if the lock didn't hold?

Panic swept away all tact and strategy she might have used.

"I don't want to talk to you, now or ever. Go away, Mike. Stay away. I mean it. This is the end. Do you understand?"

"I want you!"

"Go away!"

"I'll die if I can't have you!"

The door rattled again. The lock was old and rusted. Betty was trembling with fear. Should she call for help? Should she phone the Dunns and ask them to pick her up? How could she explain all this to them—they were too happily married and too Christian to understand the mess she'd gotten herself into. As a matter of fact, she didn't really understand it herself.

Her encounter with Mike in Wiesbaden had been quite warmhearted, improperly so, but she hadn't been married then. And in no way had he acted so aggressively. Of course, he'd known that Jon was nearby and that the world, in a sense, was watching. Her reunion with Jon had been a news story, and Mike was well aware of the vigilance of the media.

In Kiev there was no media. There was no Jon. There was no escape, no place to hide. For all she knew he was shadowing her night and day—he was perfectly capable of doing so. This was an eerie, dangerous situation. And Mike's behavior verged upon madness.

The door was perfectly still. All was quiet now. Had he left? Was he trying to figure out how to pick the lock?

"Lord, protect me." She spoke the prayer again and again, quite sure God was too disgusted with her to answer. She was certainly disgusted with herself. She waited, almost afraid to move. Was he outside? Was he coming back?

Day followed a long, sleepless night. Sunday morning came with the twittering of birds and an innocent light that mocked the horror of the night before. Betty got up and headed for the shower, wishing the water were hot enough to wash away the indecency she felt. She looked in the bathroom mirror, and a whore stared back at her—an unfaithful, fickle whore.

"Jon, I'm sorry," she spoke to the wind that blew in through the outside window. "I think, this time, I've learned my lesson.

"God," she continued her communication with unseen beings, "I pray he never knows. Please forgive me and don't ever let Jon know."

Aware that Mike might very well be stalking her, she decided to go to the hotel next door for breakfast. She took a cab, and watched to see if anyone followed her. A rank amateur at espionage, she nevertheless determined that the coast was clear.

Settled in the relative luxury of the Intourist Hotel's restaurant, she nibbled at a cube of soft, white cheese sprinkled with coarse sugar. The coffee was tolerable, and she began to relax. Then it occurred to her that Mike might be staying in the hotel. Alarmed, she paid for her food and tried to decide where to go and what to do.

Sightseeing. He'll never find me if I'm sightseeing. Shaky and unsure of what her next steps should be, she rushed into the Intourist office at the hotel. "I want to go sightseeing," she explained breathlessly to the neatly dressed woman behind the desk. "Could you help me hire a driver?"

"Yes, of course." The woman made a call and rapidly concluded some sort of arrangements. After agreeing on a price, which Betty gladly paid with a neat pile of rubles, the Intourist woman asked, "What do you want to see?"

"Well, I've already been to that old monastery," she answered.

"Pechera Lavra?"

"Is that the one with the catacombs?"

The woman nodded, and Betty babbled on, rather apologetically, "I don't know what else there is. I should have done more reading about Kiev before I came. And since I got here, I've been too busy to find out."

The woman, probably a displaced Moscovite, exhibited no civic pride. She simply shrugged. "I'll tell the driver to go to the usual places."

A tattered green Mercedes pulled up a few minutes later, and Betty got in, again glancing around to see if anyone was watching. The driver spoke almost no English, and Betty quickly reviewed her Russian vocabulary, which was limited to "Spasibo," "Da," and "Nyet."

You should have said nyet to Mike the day you got here, she castigated herself, wondering how and when her nightmare would end. By now her fear had broadened beyond the threat of Jon's finding out about Mike, or of Mike calling her in Laguna Beach after she got home. Considering the night before, she was thinking more in terms of rape. Or physical abuse. Or even murder. Fear was riding in the back seat with her and wasn't about to leave.

"War Memorial." The driver spoke the words carefully, interrupting a horrible stream of consciousness. She nodded, pulled her camera out of her purse, and got out of the car.

With a quick glance behind her, she walked toward a marble statue that was heavily festooned with wreaths and flowers. Several brides and grooms stood in front of it, having their pictures taken. *Must be some sort of a local tradition*, she reasoned.

She watched them come and go in old black cars that wore matching wedding-ring decorations above the windshield. Her own wedding, just over a year before, drifted into her mind. Ice-blue silk and pearls. Prayers and promises. She remembered the high hopes she and Jon had shared for a perfect life together and the poem she had written, which Jon had read at the reception.

> For our fears, give us courage
> In our tears, find a song.
> For our doubts, grant conviction,
> Where we're weak, make us strong.

Shame washed over her in filthy waves. Grieved at the sight of the happy brides and grooms, she fled back to the Mercedes with a guilty petition in her heart. *God, I'm sorry. I've failed again. And I'm in the worst mess of my life. Please help me. And please answer the prayer of that poem I wrote. It isn't too late, is it?*

"Go?" the driver inquired, gesturing toward the road.

"Yes. Da." Betty, answered. "Go."

A few minutes later, the car pulled into a heavily shaded paved area. Betty looked out the window and saw a domed, churchlike structure.

"St. Vladimir," the driver said, nodding. "Big church."

Again Betty got out of the car, leaving her driver smoking and reading a thick book with an undecipherable cover. She walked toward the entrance. A couple of scarved old women in knitted sweaters glanced at her as she walked in with them. One of them pointed to the camera in her hand and frowned, moving her index finger back and forth and shaking her head.

Betty complied and put the camera back into her purse. She went through the door. In doing so, she found herself in another world. An Orthodox Sunday morning service was in progress, and she was about to be a participant, whether she intended to or not.

The vast, echoing building was packed with worshipers, most of whom were on their knees. There were no seats; everyone either stood or kneeled. A pure tenor voice was singing a perfect line of music. The priest's solo was answered by a choir in an upstairs loft behind her, so pure in tone that it brought tears to Betty's eyes.

The church was ablaze with candlelight. Every icon, and there seemed to be hundreds of them, had a vast array of slender, amber-colored candles lit in front of it. Countless bouquets of roses and other summer flowers, offerings from the poor, breathed their fragrance into the heavy air.

A little counter, unobtrusively placed near the doorway, sold the tapers for next to nothing. Realizing that they represented prayers, Betty bought two—one to express her need for protection and another to plead for reconciliation with Jon. Tearfully, she lit them off already-burning wicks and set them in empty holders.

She couldn't comprehend a word of the haunting liturgy, although its form reminded her of the Episcopal prayer book readings she had so treasured just months before. Golden carvings and vibrant paintings of Christ's life and death, of vast heavenly hosts, and of beloved Bible stories surrounded her. The music was almost angelic. The humility of the simple people around her was compelling.

She got on her knees and began to whisper her own prayers in her own language.

"God, I've sinned against you, and I'm not sure how it happened."

"In your anger do not sin": Do not let the sun go down while you're still angry, and do not give the devil a foothold.

Without benefit of a sermon, Betty finally understood the Lord's word to her. The liturgy continued, its rich harmony uninterrupted by her thoughts.

Her two candle-prayers were hard at work, pleading with heaven on her behalf.

Her body was in a posture of submission, and the cold, stone floor beneath her knees did not diminish her desire to humble herself. And at last, because it was God's time to reveal His truth to her, she began to understand.

You did not sin by speaking angry words or by becoming violent or rude or rough.

You sinned by letting the sun go down on your wrath day after day, week after week.

You continued in your anger against your husband, because it hid your own pain from you, and it made you feel strong.

You rejected compassion, forgiveness, and mercy, because they would have forced you to fully experience your hurt and disappointment.

If you had chosen to be forgiving, you could have depended on My strength.

Instead you chose to depend on your own bitterness, and your bitterness hardened your heart.

In your anger, you gave the Enemy an opportunity to destroy your life and the lives of others.

If you had forgiven Jon, told him of your hurt, and tried to understand him, Mike Brody would have sickened you immediately.

But his flattery appealed to you because you had hardened your heart against your husband.

"God, it's all true. I repent. I'm sorry, and I pray that You'll forgive me."

The heavenly choir seemed to be building to a

crescendo. She looked around briefly. Kneeling believers remained in place, heads bowed, lips moving.

"What do I do now? Is it too late?"

Forgive Jon.

"I do forgive him. I've already forgiven him. Whatever he did wrong, I forgive him. And Lord, You forgive him, too. Maybe he used poor judgment, or whatever. But I've been ten times worse than he has. Forgive *me*, Lord."

You are already forgiven. Now forgive yourself.

Betty glanced around again. Her eyes rested on a crucifix. The wretched form that hung upon it looked shrunken, so large was the cross. All her life, Betty had been taught to disdain the crucifix—it represented the Roman church and a dead Christ. She, a cradle Protestant, was supposed to worship a living Lord.

But in the sanctity of that holy place, she accepted something for the first time. That withered-looking form, hanging on a wooden cross, wasn't just a religious symbol of a dead Jesus. That crumpled body embodied the entirety of her sin—past, present, and future. It also represented her imperfect, unfulfilled desires, fallen victim to the world's immense cruelty.

There on the cross hung her dream of a happy marriage. Her longing to be wholeheartedly loved. Her constant failure to measure up: stupid mistakes, willful rebellions, and foolish choices. Every loss of her lifetime was nailed there, dead and cold and lifeless.

She began to weep, bitterly and without hope. In that Kiev church, thousands of miles from home and loved ones, the blackness of Calvary overtook her. Sobbing with despair, she covered her face with her hands, ashamed and alone.

And then, for a reason she could neither fathom nor recall, Betty suddenly remembered the Resurrection.

All at once, she looked up and scanned the throng as if someone had spoken her name. Music continued to swell. Murmuring prayers persisted. Nothing in the few seconds of her spiritual revelation had changed in the candlelit room surrounding her. But her inner world had been set ablaze by the touch of an unseen Hand. Betty had instantaneously recognized that the stone had been rolled away from the tomb. And the all-powerful One who had moved it was still at work in the world.

Just then some change took place around her. People were rising from their knees and moving toward the center of the sanctuary. Betty wanted desperately to take communion with them there, right then, but she wasn't sure if it was appropriate for her to do so. Rising stiffly to her feet, she suddenly felt out of place and self-conscious. She was at least a foot taller than most of the babushkas standing near her, and her hands were black with mascara. She could only imagine what her face looked like.

Loath to draw further attention to herself, she slipped quietly out the door and headed for the green Mercedes. The driver soon deposited her at the top of a hill, where the Motherland statue reigned. Around the towering woman's feet were frescoes depicting the heroism of the Ukrainian people during the Nazi invasion of 1941. Betty found a quiet place to sit.

World War II history was of no interest to her at the moment. She simply wanted to think, pray, and avoid going back to the hotel as long as possible. The carvings that surrounded her were hewn from grim, dark stone. They were brightened here and there by scarlet-ribboned bouquets, lovingly placed in memory of loved ones who had fallen at the hands of stormtroopers more than fifty years before.

Life and death. Death and life. A deep, shuddering sigh filled her lungs, and she consciously tried to breathe out every vestige of her fears. The blessing of St. Vladimir's service was with her to stay, but there were practical issues to be addressed. She began to rack her brain for answers and solutions.

A thought intruded on her reasoning. *Trust in the LORD with all your heart and lean not on your own understanding.*

Fighting the impulse to piously reply with a variation of "God helps them that help themselves," she concluded that her own understanding hadn't been of much use to her thus far anyway. Submitting to the Hand that had touched her so gently, she felt unexplainably protected. Relieved and determined to stay that way, she made a conscious decision to relax for the rest of the day, to enjoy Kiev's many points of interest, and to eliminate her fears about Mike Brody until further notice.

That night, locking herself into her room, Betty was strangely calm. Her newfound peace of mind was definitely the kind of peace "that passes understanding." In fact, it made no sense. Nothing gave her reason to believe that Mike wouldn't be back, obsessive as ever, hoping to shake the door down. Yet she remained detached and unconcerned.

Of the several emotions she might have identified that night—hope, serenity, relief—the most overwhelming of all was gratitude. She had somehow caught a glimpse of an all-new salvation, not just one that would rescue her from a distant lake of fire, but also from a hellish existence on planet earth in the here and now. Believing herself to be the most foolish of all females, Betty felt she deserved the worst life had to offer. And yet that dying-living man-God had saved her, not just once, but time and again. She couldn't allow herself to doubt that He would continue to do so until she finally entered the world to come.

Trying to record her thankfulness, and remembering another foolish woman in another time and place, she began to write.

> Him again,
> Reclining with the others.
> "Uncommon," she murmured,
> "And I thought I'd seen them all."
> Then He smiled,
> Eyes alight with friendship.
>
> It was enough.
>
> "This time *I* will buy,"
> She vowed, rushing to find her priceless flask.
> Recklessly she shattered it,
> Fragrant oil spilling across dusty feet.
> Weeping, then giddy with delight,
> She curled her hair around His ankles,
> And wove it between His toes.
>
> Foolish, wicked, wasteful whore!
> No love ever touched Him more.

Satisfied with her offering of praise, Betty glanced at the clock. It was after 9:30. Not a word from Mike—so far. Would the silence continue through the night? She brushed her teeth, turned out the lights, and climbed into bed.

Having slept so little the night before, it wasn't five minutes before sleep overtook her. And it wasn't an hour before loud knocking at her door awakened her.

"Oh, God, no!" she whispered out loud. She could hardly breathe, so intense was her terror. Despite her pleas to heaven, the knocking continued. Shaking and stunned, she moved closer to the door, trying to hear if anything was being said.

"Betty?"

At first she drew back in horror. It was a quiet voice. It didn't sound like Mike's, but she wasn't about to answer. If she did, he'd know for sure that she was inside.

"Betty? Are you in there?"

That's not Mike. "Who is it?" she answered, fear quivering in her voice.

"It's me. Jon! Open up!"

It can't be Jon. He's in Laguna. How can he be here? What if it's a trick?

"Are you sure it's you? What are you doing here?"

"Who else would it be? I came to be with you, of course." The voice was clearly Jon's.

Betty unlocked the door, and there stood her husband. He was crisscrossed with carry-on luggage straps, and the hallway outside the room was littered with cameras and clothes bags. He looked as if he hadn't slept or shaved for a week. Although unsmiling, he was gazing at her earnestly, and his arms were open wide, waiting to embrace her.

And in that very miraculous moment, that's all Betty needed to know.

9

Exhausted as he was, Jon wouldn't rest until he had recounted the details of his agony to his wife. First, he told her how shattered he had been by her poem, how it had grieved him to find not a single word of friendly greeting from her upon his return from the Yukon. "How could you leave me without saying good-bye? I didn't understand how you could do that—until I read your poem. I must have read and reread it a hundred times, Betty. I'm sorry. Please forgive me."

Momentarily speechless and aware of the truth behind Jon's words, Betty shook her head silently and stared at her hands.

He told her that he wanted to make things right between them, of his determination to come to Kiev, and about the immense difficulties he had faced in trying to get there. The endless delays. The unexplainable frustrations. The heartbreaking fear that he had permanently lost her.

Finally, with such intensity as she had never seen in him, he said, "We have to make several very significant changes in our marriage. And we're going to start with the way we communicate. We have *got* to talk to each other, Betty, no matter how upset we feel. You've got to talk to me, and I've got to talk to you. If we think we're avoiding confrontations by keeping our resentments to ourselves, we are very foolish indeed. We've very nearly destroyed our marriage by refusing to be honest with each other. It's got to change—and I mean *now*—from this moment on. Do you understand? Don't you agree?"

Betty studied Jon's face in amazement. It was stern, although unabashedly streaked with tears. There was no soft, gentle pleading in his voice; he used no diplomatic phrases. Everything about him exuded genuine love and concern. He was looking into her eyes. "Do you understand?" he asked again, doggedly waiting for an answer.

"Jon, it was all my fault. I've known that for several days. I asked God to forgive me in church today." Her words were barely audible. "I was bitter about things that happened and even about things that didn't happen— things I imagined. I built up a case against you in my mind and then refused to forgive you. Now all I can do is ask *you* to forgive *me*." Her voice trembled and her body shook. "It was all my fault . . ."

"Don't take all the blame. It was *our* fault. Both of us were playing the same game. Don't fault yourself any more than you fault me. Just tell me this: Will you promise to talk to me from now on when you're upset? I promise to talk to you and to sort things out on the spot, no matter how hard it is. Will you promise?"

He looked at her searchingly. "If we don't promise to change," he added, "I don't think our marriage will survive."

"I promise," she nodded, almost childlike in her response. Impulsively she put her arms around him, clinging to him, in great need of his embrace. This was a different Jon than she'd ever known before, powerful and determined. She was grateful for his strength and somewhat awed by his demeanor. As for Betty herself, she felt like a wornout rag doll—wide-eyed and limp and inadequate.

"I'm sorry," was the last thing she said that night before they both collapsed into a dreamless sleep. And those two words bore more weight of meaning than Jon would ever know, both in their sincerity and in the expanse of their apology. Betty's regret was immense. Her sorrow was overwhelming. Her repentance was complete.

Morning found Jon and Betty clinging to each other for dear life. They were lying in the same narrow bed, both of them intently trying not to land in a heap on the wooden floor. Glad as they were to be together, the sleeping arrangements at the Hotel Rus weren't especially conducive to romantic reunions.

Jon's tone was considerably less authoritative that morning, but he wasn't exactly thrilled with his surroundings. "This has got to be the worst hotel on earth, Betty. Why didn't you move to a better one?"

"I never even thought about it. I figured I had to stay here if this is where Kramer wanted me to be."

Jon got out of bed, rubbed his scruffy face, and went into the bathroom. "There's no hot water," he reported after a couple of minutes. "It's barely lukewarm."

"I know."

"Betty, get your stuff together. We're moving out of here! I don't care what Kramer says, this place is a disgrace. What time are the Dunns supposed to pick you up?"

"They'll be here at ten. Boy, are they going to be surprised to see you."

"Have you been in the hotel next door?"

"The Intourist? Yes. It's a lot better, at least as far as the restaurant is concerned."

"Well, it couldn't be worse. They can help us move over there before we go to the hospital."

"Are you sure it's okay to do that?" *Please say yes. Mike will never find me there.*

"Betty, I'll handle Kramer if he gives us any trouble."

A sudden and enormous thwacking sound came from the bathroom. "Good Lord! Have you been keeping a cockroach tally?"

"Three. Or maybe the same one three times. It lives in there by the mirror."

"Not any more," Jon said replacing his shoe.

Trying not to laugh, Betty got out the hot pot so he could shave and she could make coffee.

He smiled fondly at her diligence. "You'll make the best of anything, won't you?"

No, I make the worst messes on earth. "I'm so glad you're here, Jon. I just couldn't believe it was you last night."

"I've never had so much trouble getting anywhere in my life. I felt like the devil himself was blocking the way."

Maybe he was.

Jon was rummaging in his kit, looking for his razor. "Did I tell you I flew in here with a guy from the American Embassy in Moscow? He's some kind of investigator. He'd been drinking and told me some things he probably shouldn't have. But he says an agent was found dead yesterday morning in the Dniepro Hotel."

By that time Jon was shaving in earnest and Betty was rustling around in the closet, trying to find something to wear. She froze. Her hands turned to ice. She carefully cleared her throat, not trusting her voice. "What kind of an agent was he?"

"Well, from what the guy told me, it must have been a CIA type. He was over here supposedly following up on some Middle East problem. They think maybe he was AWOL or something. I guess he'd lied on a couple of reports, and they didn't know what he was up to. Anyway, his death was set up to look like a suicide. Or maybe it was a suicide, nobody seems to be sure. The poor guy had fallen out of a window. They don't know if he jumped, lost his balance, or got a shove from somebody else. That's what the man from the embassy was coming here to find out."

Betty could almost hear Mike's voice, hoarse and desperate, speaking through the door. *I'll die if I can't have you!*

Her heart was pounding against her chest and thundering in her ears. Involuntarily, she sat down on the bed—for the moment, her legs were unwilling to support her weight. She cleared her throat again. "That's horrible, Jon! Uh, did he know the agent's name?"

"No, but he told me the dead man had a wife and three kids in Virginia, and the government wants a full report together before the family is notified."

Oh, God, no! I should have known . . .

Jon continued, "Those agency guys are a strange lot, anyway. And you think I travel a lot!"

Smooth of cheek and fragrant with after shave, Jon emerged from the bathroom and took Betty in his arms. She began to cry, and Jon held her very tightly.

"Listen, I'm sorry," she murmured. "I'm sorry . . ." She was sorrier than Jon knew, more penitent than she would ever be able to tell him.

"Betty, don't cry. I was wrong, too. We're going to work all this out together. It's no more your fault than mine. Look, I want to show you something . . ."

Jon pulled a Bible out of his suitcase and opened it to the verse in Jeremiah he had read in Anchorage. Betty wiped her eyes with her hand and forced her mind to focus on whatever it was Jon was reading: "I will give them singleness of heart and action, so that they will always fear me for their own good and the good of their children after them."

Slowly and carefully, he explained to her how God had encouraged him with that Scripture during his bleak stay in Alaska and how he'd tried to call and talk to her about it. Then in words he had rehearsed a thousand times, Jon told her the facts about Carla, about her hospitalization, her threats, and his unsuccessful attempts to shield Betty from the truth.

Betty shook her head in incredulity. "I can't believe this. I had no idea. I honestly thought you were still in love with her . . ."

"I know, Joyce told me."

When you pass through the rivers, they will not sweep over you. When you walk through the fire, you will not be burned. Thank you, Joyce.

Betty touched Jon's warm face with a shaky hand. "I had no idea, Jon. I was so blind and selfish. Again, please forgive me."

"I was blind, too, Betty. And I realized after I read this that if we were to have one heart and one way, we would have to include each other in every aspect of our lives—problems, mistakes, tough decisions, unpleasant ex-wives, everything."

Betty had started quaking as Jon told her about the agent's death. Now, although this continuation of their earlier conversation had her full attention, the inner shuddering continued unabated. "I'm sorry you couldn't reach me from Anchorage, but it wasn't intentional." She explained, her voice uneven, that the kitchen phone hadn't been hung up properly and she'd waiting all night to hear from him.

Staring at the Bible and wondering what strange spiritual fires and flood waters they had passed through, she suddenly pointed at the text. "What do you think it means, 'for the good of their children after them.'"

He laughed. "Well, what do *you* think it means? It's pretty obvious to me."

"You know, I've never thought about wanting children before, Jon, until I met Dmitry." She told him the story of the little green-eyed boy with the dream of heaven. Jon watched, astonished, as excitement animated her face. She described the sickbed scene, her unplanned prayer, and the miraculous transformation of the following morning.

"I can't wait for you to meet him. He's got a special quality—I don't know what it is."

As they packed their bags and got ready to leave the hotel, Betty couldn't escape the sickness that gripped her every time she pondered the horrible story of the dead agent. Was it—could it possibly be—Mike Brody? Had he been a married man and a father all along? *Nothing would surprise me. There is nothing I could hear about Mike that would surprise me.*

Brody hadn't called or showed up since Saturday night. God willing, he wouldn't reappear while Jon was around. Still, was it possible that he was dead? It was a terrible thought, no matter how formidable he had become. How could she ever know? There was no logical way for her to find out. One thing she knew very well: It was entirely possible that something had snapped in Mike's mind—his behavior had been erratic all along.

Jon was in the shower, and she was staring out the window across the vast, empty Dinamo Stadium. A cosmic puzzle bewildered her—the shocking duality of her own nature. In two days, two lives had been deeply impacted by her beliefs and behavior.

She had prayed for a desperately sick child. She had done so without ulterior motive only because she loved the boy and had felt urged by an inner impulse to seek God's help on his behalf. Her prayer had apparently touched a source of life that had budded and then burst into bloom within Dmitry, enlivening his tiny, tortured frame. The boy, his mother Sophia, the Dunns, and everyone else involved had seen the evidence of some irresistible life, vital enough to swallow up, at least for a time, the encroaching specter of death.

Yet Betty had trifled with the mind of a sick man in a gloomy display that equaled any goodheartedness Dmitry's miracle had authenticated. She had enabled him to reveal glimpses of dark, intimate fantasies he hid from others. In her self-serving ignorance, she had led him into some cavern of obsession he had concealed even from himself, perhaps driving him into more madness than he could bear.

Life and death. Death and life.

The dichotomy was unbearable. Fortunately, Betty's weighty thoughts were interrupted by Jon's frenetic activity. He was determined to get the Surrey-Dixons, bag and baggage, out of the Hotel Rus by ten o'clock. Come life or death, hell or high water, they would be checked out.

Another interference also tempered Betty's philosophical despair. Somewhere in the recesses of her mind she heard the voice of what might well have been a practical, cautious angel: *Don't take too much credit for Dmitry or Mike*, the being said. *You aren't nearly as important as you might like to think.*

When the Dunns arrived, Betty rushed out to greet—and prepare—them. "You'll never believe who's here! My husband! Jon arrived last night!"

Marian was gratified and rather intrigued by the soft light shining through Betty's countenance. Mrs. Jon Surrey-Dixon looked more relaxed and far less laden with care than she had in recent days. As Jon and Steven discussed the necessity of changing hotels and began to load up the baggage, Betty put her hand on Marian's arm.

"I've got to talk to you."

"Is everything all right?"

"Well, yes and no. It's a wonderful miracle that Jon's here, and the Lord really touched me even before he came. I want to tell you all about that. But Marian, I'm afraid something terrible has happened to Mike."

"Like what?"

"Like, he might be dead."

Marian's face paled, and before the two women could continue their dialogue, Jon and the doctor were getting in the car, and they were all on their way to the Intourist Hotel. Although it was "next door" in a strict sense, a car could not be driven from the Hotel Rus entrance to the Hotel Intourist entry without traversing several city blocks, which Steven did without complaint.

"We should have insisted on putting you here ourselves," Marian commented apologetically, looking around at the newer, more tidy surroundings.

"I didn't want to make waves with Ed Kramer," Betty answered, "But Jon couldn't stand it at the Rus."

"He's right. Ed Kramer has always been very kind to us, but he is a bit of a penny-pincher, I'm afraid."

Their much larger room in the Intourist was spotless, crisp white trimmed in dark wood, with a small balcony, a refrigerator, and an immaculate bathroom. Betty sighed with relief. "We've only got a few more days, but at least we won't be battling roaches."

"Or drunks," Marian volunteered sagely.

"Or old friends," Betty whispered, with Jon safely out of hearing.

With Jon and Betty's luggage securely stowed in the new room, the foursome headed for the hospital. Steven took Jon on a quick tour, while Betty and Marian retreated to the office.

"Why do you think Mike could be dead?" Marian got straight to the point, realizing they had little time to talk.

Betty recounted what Jon had learned on his flight from Moscow to Kiev and included the story of Mike's door-rattling visitation on Saturday night.

Marian shuddered. "Betty! You should have called us— I told you to call! I hate to say it, but from the sound of things, you've been rescued from a very dangerous man."

Betty's eyes met Marian's. "I'm so ashamed, Marian. I was so stupid. I was just enjoying his attention and subconsciously paying Jon back, I guess. I didn't realize what he was up to. But, naive or not, I feel like a tramp for what I did."

Marian touched her friend's arm soothingly. "Betty, you could have done a lot worse. Do you remember what I told you the other day, that Steven and I had some very rocky days at the beginning of our marriage?"

"Yes, but it couldn't have been this bad!"

"Betty, I had an affair with another man when Steven and I had been married for less than a year. Then, just about the time I was ready to repent, I found out that Steven was sleeping with one of the nurses at the hospital!"

Betty was stunned. Neither Steven nor his stocky, salt-and-pepper-haired wife looked the least bit like philanderers. *It's pretty tough to imagine them in bed with each other, much less with anybody else.* "That's unbelievable. How on earth did you manage to work things out? You seem so happy now."

"We are very happy now, Betty, happier than almost any couple I know. But that's what I wanted to tell you the other day. It hasn't been effortless by any stretch of the imagination. Right at the start we had to forgive each other. We had to rebuild trust and stop being angry. And then we had to forge a relationship that was meant to endure—no matter what. Nothing about our marriage has been easy or spontaneous. And for the first five or six years, it was hard work, it was emotionally exhausting, and it seemed like we'd never get it right."

"Why was it so hard?"

"Partly because we believed, up until we got into trouble, that it was just supposed to work all by itself. I expected Steven to read my mind, and he thought I should read his. I believed the old adage, 'Love is enough,' and Steven thought 'Love means never having to say you're sorry.' Worst of all, we thought because we were Christians that we were guaranteed a happy ending. I guess you can imagine that two extramarital affairs pretty well popped that bubble."

They could hear the men's voices coming down the hall. Marian impulsively put her hand around Betty's. "Shakespeare once wrote, 'Know thyself, and it must follow, as the night the day, thou canst not then be false to any man.' If you prefer Scripture, remember David's words, 'Search me, O God, and know my heart; test me and know my anxious thoughts,' In both cases, the message is personal *truth*—in the inner person."

Betty nodded. "I was lying to myself about the anger inside me, and that's how I got into trouble."

"Some people call it denial. Whatever it is, may the dear Lord in heaven keep us all in truth and forever out of dishonesty." Marian remarked beseechingly, glancing toward the men's approaching footsteps. "And don't worry unduly about Mike. It's a terrible possibility, but God is in control of our living and dying. He knows what He's doing."

"Do you think I should tell Jon?"

Marian thought for a moment, then shook her head. "It was your lesson, Betty, and no one else needs to know about it. You've confessed it to me and to the Lord, right?"

"Right."

"Well, then, I think the Lord would simply say to you, 'Go and sin no more.'"

The boy's green eyes were glowing with excitement. He knew before a word was said who Jon was and why he was there.

"Dmitry, I want you to meet my husband Jon. Jon, this is my friend Dmitry."

Marian began her job of translating with those words. And Dmitry responded with a laugh. "He is like you."

"What do you mean."

"I mean you are the same."

Jon and Betty glanced at each other.

One heart, one way.

"Dmitry, I want you to tell Jon about heaven."

Dmitry's face gleamed as he related his dream to his new friend. His mother, who looked younger every time Betty saw her, beamed as he spoke. No one in the room doubted that they were receiving firsthand news from another world. Jon snapped several pictures as Dmitry reported his adventure, artfully framing the boy in his viewfinder along with Sophia and Dr. Dunn.

"A couple more with you, Betty," Jon directed, moving her next to the bed.

As he continued to click the lens, Jon said, "Dmitry, I'm going to promise you something, okay?"

"Okay, what is it, Mr. Jon."

"When my wife and I have our first son, we will call him Dmitry. Do you understand?"

"You will have a son, and his name will be Dmitry." The boy spoke the words with such certainty that when Marian began to translate them, she looked at him in surprise.

"He means 'if,' doesn't he?" Betty laughed.

"He doesn't mean 'if.' He is saying 'you *will* have a son,' and don't argue with Dmitry. You should know that by now."

Just as they were leaving the room, Dmitry called Betty back. "I did not like your other friend. He was not like you." With that, he brightened, put his arms around her neck, and added, "Tomorrow I go home with my mother."

Sophia nodded, her brown eyes aglitter with hope and excitement. "*Spasibo*," she said, holding Betty's hand in both of hers. "Thank God . . . ," she managed to say in English.

"Thank God," Betty repeated, wondering what the future held for Dmitry, the wonderful boy who loved to talk about heaven.

That night, Betty and Jon sat alone in the restaurant at the Intourist Hotel. "I brought something with me," Jon suddenly remembered, reaching inside his jacket. He pulled out the Victoria's Secret package and the anniversary card.

Betty, recognizing the parcel, looked at him rather gravely. "That was a bad night for me, Jon," she ventured, trying out her new resolution to be as truthful as possible without making huge waves.

"I knew that when I found this. And I want you to

know that that situation was my fault—entirely my fault. You can't blame yourself for any part of it."

She looked at the table, trying to think of some way to rescue him. "I could have waited up for you . . ."

"Betty," Jon said quietly, "let me be wrong. Don't take responsibility for everything."

"Jon, let's just forget it. We've both learned a lesson, haven't we?"

"Well, there's one thing I'd like to do before we get home."

"What?"

"I want to have another honeymoon."

"Another honeymoon? How? Where?"

"In London, where we meant to go in the first place. Hawaii was wonderful, but we lost so much of the beauty in all the misunderstandings. Let's try again."

"Jon, did you ever love Carla?" Betty's non sequitur response nearly caused him to forget what he'd just said.

He scrutinized her, first in confusion, and then in the full realization that she had to have an answer, once and for all. And it had to be the truth. *It's been worrying her since Hawaii*, he suddenly understood.

"Betty, I was very physically attracted to Carla. She was a sexy, voluptuous girl when we met. She came on very strong to me, I responded to her with more than enough enthusiasm. Does that hurt you?"

After what I've just done? Are you kidding? "I understand."

"Carla and I never talked about anything but ourselves and other people. And her moods quickly took away any pleasure I derived from our sex life. Did I love her? I don't think so now, but I guess I did then, or I wouldn't have married her."

"And that's it?"

"That's it. She's not very attractive these days. I think if you knew her you'd feel more pity than jealousy. She's no threat to you. She's just a sad, confused woman who needs our prayers."

There was a pause that lasted no more than ten seconds. "Okay, we can go to London."

Jon shook his head. Then, for lack of anything better to do, he laughed rather loudly.

In the days that followed, he had more than enough to keep himself busy, catching up with Betty's interviews, reading her material, and trying to capture the same images on film she'd painstakingly sketched out in her rough notes. By the end of the week, all the film would have to be used because they were scheduled to leave for Moscow on Sunday night and for London on Monday morning.

Steven and Marian Dunn wanted very much to spend an entire evening with the Surrey-Dixons. And now that Betty had removed them from their hallowed pedestals, she was more inclined to want to chat with them, too.

"Why don't you let us take you to a restaurant?" Jon suggested.

Steven nodded. "Well, we could do that, but it's nice to visit at home sometimes. Not so noisy, you know."

On Friday night the foursome gathered at the Dunns' tiny, deliciously fragrant apartment. They moved the wooden chairs into the sitting room, turned on the London Symphony cassette, and began to eat and talk.

Marian, as usual, led the way. She wanted to initiate a discussion about married life. She sensed in Jon and Betty the potential for a deep and satisfying lifetime union, but she was still concerned about one critical issue: careers vs. conjugal bliss.

Coincidentally, Marian Dunn and Harold Fuller had virtually the same point of view with regards to the Surrey-Dixon marriage. Of course, Harold's perspective was affected by his own myopic devotion to Lucilla and his belief that she had surely been the most perfect wife in the history of Western civilization. Lucilla had stayed home, so all wives should stay home. She had cooked and cleaned compulsively. So should every other woman on the planet. Naturally the fact that Lucilla couldn't drive and enjoyed the company of very few people had limited her movements considerably. But what was that to Harold?

Additionally, Harold's use of weary aphorisms could not match Marian's well-honed application of the language. He, for example, might speak of birds of a feather flocking together. Marian would probably cite peer groups identified by their common interests, educational echelons, and background. But those two strangers, never having met or spoken, both felt that Jon and Betty had better find a way to spend time together, and lots of it, or they would surely shipwreck during some future storm.

"How difficult would it be for you to find projects you could develop as a team?" Marian asked them between mouthfuls of homemade vegetable soup.

Jon reported rather smugly that he'd already been looking into that possibility. "I've contacted a couple of editors, and I think we could sell several ideas to some publishers. It's just a matter of saying no to a few jobs and holding out for the projects we can coproduce."

"How do you feel about that, Betty?"

Betty hardly took time to consider her answer, and what she said was the exact opposite of what she really felt. In response to Marian's knowledgeable air, a defiant feeling was creeping into her body. No way was she going to give Marian—or Harold—an inch of ground. "I feel like Jon and I are both talented, and we don't want to hold each other back with our desire to be together."

Steven looked at her curiously. "What's first priority, then?"

"What do you mean?"

"I mean marriage or talent?"

Betty looked at Jon a little uncertainly. She really wanted to say 'marriage,' but, on the other hand, she didn't like the way the conversation was going. "I think we can have it both ways. Some projects together and some separately."

"What about you, Jon?"

"Naturally I'd like to work with Betty every chance I get, but I can't very well scuttle all my own contacts and opportunities or we'll starve. Besides, I love my work. I don't want to stop covering important news stories."

Betty, having subdued her burst of rebellion, tried a different tack. "I think the commitment we have in our hearts is more important than where we're located physically. Sure, we shouldn't be apart all the time—that's not what we want anyway. But if we can't be together, we have to be completely devoted to each other, no matter who comes along or what happens along the way."

Don't look at me that way, Marian.

Jon nodded, fully in agreement with Betty's words. "I think it's wonderful that the two of you can live here and work together every day. It's the way God has taken care of you. But I'm not sure that everybody has to fit the same mold. Maybe we should let Him into the process."

The Dunns never really felt that they'd won Jon and Betty over to their point of view, but they were gracious enough hosts to leave the issue on the table. "They'll learn," they assured themselves, "and maybe they won't make the same mistakes we did."

And the Surrey-Dixons, who thought the Dunns were very opinionated, well-intentioned, and at least partially right, concluded, "We'll probably end up working together part of the time anyway, but why make a religion out of it?"

By the time they parted, the four had found many other matters to agree upon—Bach, Shakespeare, Russian ice cream, and Dmitry's charisma being among the most obvious topics. They also unanimously concluded that Ed Kramer of Vancouver, although very nice indeed, was a bit of a spendthrift and should perhaps invest his next financial windfall in a new hairpiece.

Amidst hugs and kisses, hosts and guests said goodbye until Sunday, when the Dunns drove Jon and Betty to Borispol Airport for their Moscow flight.

"Marian, thank you for helping me through that Mike situation," Betty whispered to her as they left.

"I meant to tell you—I heard today from an American woman that the body has already been flown back to the states. Still no name, but it was a man in his thirties, brown hair and eyes . . ."

*Oh, God, it was him. It **was** him.*

". . . and apparently, they're almost sure that the man's death was accidental. They haven't completely ruled out murder, but it looks more like an accident, and it definitely wasn't suicide."

Betty breathed out a heavy burden of guilt while reeling under a equally pressing weight of horror. A friend, no matter what his character flaws, had come to a violent end, of that she was relatively sure. But the whole story of Mike Brody would never be known—not with his rather evasive Langley, Virginia, "employer" sorting out the details. Nevertheless, Betty felt mildly vindicated. *At least I didn't singlehandedly drive him crazy.*

Later that night, Betty sat on the bed, organizing and reorganizing her luggage while Jon tinkered with film canisters, lens caps, and an astonishing array of filters. Moving some clean clothes from one bag to another, Betty came upon the crucifix she had purchased at Pachera Lavra. *I forgot all about it . . . God, You wanted me to buy this, didn't You?*

"Look, Jon. I hope you don't mind if we hang this up at home."

"Why would I mind? I'm Catholic. Remember?"

She nodded absently, distracted by her discovery. "You know, when I bought this, it was just an artifact to me, a souvenir of Kiev, 'the cradle of Christianity in Europe.' But something happened the other day in a cathedral here, and for the first time in my life I think I'm beginning to understand just what this crucifix really means."

She tried to express herself but felt she could never quite communicate to Jon the supernatural revelation she'd experienced at St. Vladimir's Cathedral. "You know, it's kind of a tourist attraction as well as a church. Why don't we go there tomorrow? I want you to see it with me."

"I'd love to see it. Maybe I can get some pictures for Kramer."

"You can take pictures outside, but they don't allow cameras inside. It's too . . . I don't know. I guess it's just too sacred for that."

The following morning, after a leisurely breakfast, they hired a car and asked to be driven to St. Vladimir's. From the outside, its array of domes and cupolas was impressive, but not awe-inspiring.

He'll probably be disappointed—I made too big a deal out of it. Oh, Lord, I want him to feel what I felt. Please help him understand.

They walked through the door together, hand in hand.

No service was in progress, although candles still gleamed and flowers lay in fresh profusion in front of the various icons. A massive depiction of Mary and the infant Jesus dominated the huge, vacant building, an image Betty had somehow failed to see the Sunday before. Other frescoes and murals, gilded and lavishly painted, captured the Last Supper and the crucifixion.

"I lit two candles last Sunday, Jon. One of them was a prayer for my safety in that awful hotel. *Enough said.* The other was for us—for our marriage. God's already answered them both, hasn't He?"

"Of course He has. But what happened here, Betty, that touched you so deeply?"

Betty pointed to a crucifix. "Well, it's kind of hard to explain. See, I realized that the form hanging there on the cross wasn't just Jesus."

Jon looked at her as if she had decided to start a new religion. "It wasn't just Jesus?"

I'm never going to be able to explain this to anybody.

"What I mean is, it was Him, but it was Him and me, too. It was Him dying for my failures. For my failure to be a good wife to you. It was Him dying for my bitterness and for my disappointment and all the rest of the things I did wrong. And then, all of a sudden, the Lord reminded me that He is alive and that my hope for the future is just as alive as He is." Betty looked at Jon's face, hoping to see a look of total and complete comprehension. She wasn't sure she did.

Okay, okay. Never mind. You had to be there.

"Let's light a couple of candles together," Jon volunteered, moving toward the counter manned by a bearded priest. All at once a small woman, obviously a nun, walked over to Betty and pointed at the gold cross Betty always wore around her neck.

Are you trying to sell me something?

Unable to comprehend what the old lady wanted, Betty frantically looked for Jon to rescue her, but his back was turned. The old nun kept pointing at the cross and even touched it a couple of times, seeming quite distressed. Betty shook her head and shrugged, assuming by now that the shrug was some sort of Slavic lingua franca.

The old nun grabbed her by the hand and led her across the room to a painting of the resurrection. There was Mary at the tomb, standing in front of the "gardener," suddenly realizing that He was, in fact, the risen Lord. "Rabboni!" Mary had cried in the old story, longing to cling to Him.

By that time Jon had rejoined Betty. "What does she want?" he whispered.

"She's trying to tell me something about the cross I'm wearing, but I'm not sure what it is." The old woman pointed to Betty's cross, to the gardener, to the open tomb, and again to Betty's cross.

All at once it made sense. The nun was trying to tell her exactly what she'd been trying to tell Jon. She nodded enthusiastically. "Yes! Da!" Betty pointed to the empty tomb. She pointed to heaven. And then she put her hand on her heart. "Jesus lives," Betty said softly in English.

"Jesu zheevoy!" Her weathered face radiant with joy, the old nun's head bobbed up and down, and she grinned toothlessly. In sheer delight, she pressed her palm against her own thin breast. "Jesu zheevoy," she nodded again and again, disappearing into the shadows. "Jesu zheevoy!"

So that's what she wanted to say: Don't wear the cross if you don't know about the Risen Christ. And we think we should send missionaries to them?

"That's what you were trying to tell me, isn't it?" Jon was clearly moved. "Unless a grain of wheat falls into the ground and dies it can bear no fruit. For something to live forever, it has to die first. Now I understand."

Betty nodded mutely. *I'm not sure I understood that part myself.*

Jon was holding two candles, and he quietly said, "Betty, I want to pray with you. I want to light this candle as a prayer that God will help you become everything He wants you to be. And if any dream of yours has died over these past few months, I pray it will live again."

He lit the first candle and placed it in a candleholder in front of the empty tomb.

"My turn." Betty took the other candle from his hand. "I pray that God will give you the desires of your heart. I pray He'll make up for all the pain you've been through. I pray that He will reward you for every month of every year that you've seen trouble and that He will establish the works of your hands."

She lit the candle, put her arm around her husband, and pressed her cheek against his chest.

"Lord," Jon prayed, "forgive us both for the pain we've caused each other. Give us one heart and one way, so that we will fear You forever, for our good and for the good of our children after us."

Then, as an afterthought, he added, "And Lord, if we ever do have a son," Jon concluded, "make him just as special and wonderful as Dmitry."

Jon and Betty stood in exquisite silence for several moments. Without a word, he bent over and kissed her very sweetly. The little nun returned just as they turned to go. She soberly put her hands on each of them and, in a language they didn't need to understand, she blessed them, sending them into the world in peace to love and serve the Lord with gladness and singleness of heart.

"Who is she, anyway?" Jon asked, an odd look on his face.

"A true believer, I guess."

That night, with Jon snoring peacefully in the background, Betty sat at the desk in their room, lost in thought.

Life and death. Death and life. Again those two immense concepts loomed in her mind, towering above all other considerations. Up until now, she had always seen them as equal powers in the world, warring against each other. But how could they be? There was no equality between them, not since that first Easter morning. Life had overcome death. Love had overcome hate. Good had overcome evil.

She smiled, fingering the golden cross at her neck. For once it seemed that joy had overcome sorrow in the heart of Elisabeth Surrey-Dixon. It was just as well. She was planning to live forever anyway.

With all that in mind, in remembrance of Mary at the tomb and the little nun and herself—pilgrim at St. Vladimir's—she wrote a poem. She was a little disappointed, because she simply could not find the words to express everything she wanted to say. However, because she'd captured at least a trace of her newfound insight, she gave it to Jon at breakfast the next morning.

> "He looks just like Him.
> *Everyone* looks like Him now,"
> She chided herself,
> Glancing at the gardener.
> "Oh, God! I'm such a fool."

"Mary!" He smiled,
Shattering the illusion.

Catching a breath of strange, new air,
She exhaled His name in wonder
And ran away chanting,
"I don't believe it!
I can't believe it!"

How dull is the earth-weary mind,
When faced with a miracle.

10

When it came time to bid the Dunns farewell, the Surrey-Dixons did so amidst promises of exchanged letters and vows of future visits.

"Thanks again for all you did for me," Betty whispered to Marian. "I'll never forget you."

"And we'll never forget what you did for Dmitry, Betty. It was God's hand, but it was your faith."

"Let's just pray he stays out of heaven for a while. I think his mother needs him down here."

With that the two couples parted, saying good-bye for what might very well amount to a lifetime.

Upon Jon and Betty's arrival from Kiev, Vnukovo Airport offered the same depressing array of sights and sounds Betty had encountered on her first sojourn there. The floor was still scummy, the cluster of departing passengers were resigned to an endless wait, and the toilets remained as smelly as ever. But this time Jon was at her side, and the value of his presence was inestimable. He wasn't much help with her baggage—he had twice as much as she. His Russian was worse than hers. But Jon was there, and when he was with Betty, her world was a better place.

"How long did you say you had to wait here for your flight to Kiev?" He looked around the terminal in distaste.

"I think it turned out to be about eight hours before we boarded. Then, after we got in the plane, we had to wait on the ground for another two."

"For what?"

"Who knows? Even if somebody had bothered to explain, I wouldn't have understood a word of it. And nobody ever explains anything, anyway. The official attitude around here is 'Nothing works right, and it's not my problem. Tough it out or go home.'"

Jon nodded his head. Regretfully, he remembered the rugged course Betty had been walking when she'd passed through Vnukovo for the first time. "If I'd known what your trip was going to be like, I would never have let you come here alone."

You can say that again.

She nodded toward a motley-looking group of men across the room. "See those guys over there? They're stoned out of their minds. And I'd swear they're the same drunks that were here three weeks ago. By the way, you never told me how long you had to wait at Vnukovo on your way to Kiev."

He smiled apologetically. "I'm sorry to tell you, but I didn't have to wait at all. I almost missed my flight, so I had to run to make the plane, but I didn't have to wait, thank God."

Marian and Steven Dunn had tentatively arranged for Ivan, a Russian acquaintance in Moscow, to drive Jon and Betty to Sheremetyevo. If he showed up, they would be spared the unpleasantries of finding a cab. Once they had accounted for their luggage, they scanned the terminal anxiously, sighting a thin, pale man holding up a mislettered sign that read "JohnBety." Grateful and relieved, they loaded themselves and their belongings in his decrepit car and settled in for the hour-long ride across Moscow.

Ivan spoke convoluted English and was exceptionally shy as well, so the car was silent as they drove along the city's outer perimeter. They had considered asking Ivan to take them to Sheremetyevo by way of Red Square, since Betty had never seen the sights there, but time was limited. Besides, it seemed unlikely that Ivan would understand their request.

Jon was apparently using the drive time to contemplate Betty's lonely journey to Kiev. Shortly after they pulled out onto the highway, with a sober look on his face, he took her hand in his and held it firmly for the duration of the journey.

She, in turn, spent the hour worrying about Mike Brody's fate.

After thanking Ivan profusely, Jon and Betty got in line for international departures at Sheremetyevo. As all good things must do, the Surrey-Dixons' tenure in the former USSR had come to an end, and the two of them were more than happy to be leaving Russia and the Ukraine behind.

"It's a good thing he drove us straight here. This is taking forever." Jon was impatiently checking his watch and the departure time printed on their tickets.

The customs process at the airport, if orderly, was infernally slow. Jon took their bags off the cart and placed them on a well-worn belt, which carried them through a historic-looking x-ray contraption. They had been standing in line for nearly half an hour when a customs agent finally looked them up and down and scrutinized his screen, all without the trace of a facial expression. He ignored every item until he saw the crucifix, which Betty had wrapped in her soiled clothing.

Suddenly, the man was energized. Like a medical researcher on the track of a new strain of virus, he eagerly zipped open a bag and yanked Betty's dirty underwear out, spreading it shamelessly all over the counter. Then with a trained and jaded eye, he examined the artifact carefully.

"Is it old?" he inquired.

"No, it's new. I bought it at the Kiev monastery." The custom official's face wore a mocking expression.

Betty glanced helplessly at Jon, and he shook his head in puzzlement. Days of religious persecution were supposedly over in Russia, but the man's visage reflected utter contempt.

"Is something wrong with the cross?" Betty inquired.

The man continued to inspect it. For a moment he appeared to be confiscating it.

"Can't I keep it?"

"What for? It's worthless," he chuckled, carelessly stuffing both the cross and her dirty clothes back into the bag.

"I guess he's still a Communist," Jon offered as they walked toward passport control.

"Maybe he's just a die-hard Protestant," Betty contended. "My father would have probably reacted the same way."

"Oh, c'mon Betty, cut out the cynicism and be nice. Your dad and I had a good talk while you were away, and he gave me some great advice. There's nothing wrong with him."

"What kind of advice?"

"Oh, he just told me to keep you pregnant and barefoot so you wouldn't get into trouble."

"My father is a narrow-minded old . . ." Betty was about to use an improper noun when the passport officer returned her documents. By the time they reached the boarding lounge, all the London-bound passengers were standing up and heading for the plane.

"Your father loves you, Betty. Whether you realize it or not."

"Right. You can have the window seat, Jon."

Jon laughed heartily, and within minutes Mr. and Mrs. Surrey-Dixon breathed a collective sigh of relief as their plane lifted off the Moscow runway and split the clouds. England would be a welcome sight indeed. Betty lifted her hands heavenward and exulted, "Hot showers, good tea, and people who speak English—here I come!"

"Do you kind of wish we were heading straight back to Laguna?" Jon was looking forward to their holiday in London, but he was well aware that she'd already been away from home for three weeks.

"You and I need to have some fun together, Jon. It was great being with you in Kiev, but it wasn't exactly a vacation."

Only one concern remained hidden in Betty's heart. In no way had she forgotten the Brody situation, not even for an hour. She'd mulled it over constantly and still wasn't sure whether she really believed Mike was dead. If he was, and it seemed highly possible, had anyone in Kiev seen them together? What if the investigation somehow included her before it was over? What if—worst of all—someone thought she had played a part in his demise?

Perhaps Betty's worst fears could be summed up in a couple of scenarios she had unhappily played and replayed in her mind during the drive from Dnukovo to Sheremetyevo. In one vignette, Jon sat reading a London tabloid. "Look at this!" he exclaimed. "You remember Mike Brody? That CIA agent you went out with in Wiesbaden? It says here he was found dead in Kiev . . ."

At that point Jon's eyes narrowed, and he sagely scrutinized Betty, a knowing look in his eyes. "Wait a minute! How could Brody have been in Kiev without your seeing him? Too much of a coincidence, Betty. You knew he was there, didn't you? And you knew he was the dead agent, right? So why didn't you tell me? I want the whole truth, Elisabeth. Speak now or forever hold your peace!"

In the other equally unpleasant scene, Jon and Betty had just returned to their London hotel room after a marvelous night at the London theater. There was a knock on the door. Outside stood two grim-faced men in suits, displaying badges. "Mrs. Surrey-Dixon? We're with the U.S. government. We're investigating the death of one of our agents, ma'am, and we'd like to have a few words with you." At that point Jon would fold his arms and cynically remark, "I should have known I couldn't trust you!"

So went the false creations proceeding from Betty's heat-oppressed brain. The worst-case scenario, of course, was that she would simply be found guilty of pushing Mike out a window and subsequently sentenced to life imprisonment without parole.

In reality, although the stench of death emanating from somewhere in the state of Virginia never quite left her, Betty kept her torturous thoughts to herself.

She felt thoroughly chastised with regards to her improper behavior in Kiev. She was fully contrite about her callousness toward Jon. But she was in no way prepared to bare her soul about the late Mike Brody to her newly reconciled husband. Marian Dunn had said, "Go, and sin no more." And so she would, with God's help, and with a firmly closed mouth.

In her view, confession might be good for the soul, but it could be disastrous to a mending marriage.

Meanwhile, with every day that passed, there was a diminished likelihood of her secret's being revealed. And those days were well spent, to be sure. Betty and Jon walked the streets of London hand in hand, seeing the sights most honeymooners only dream about. They made wishes and tossed pennies in Trafalgar Square's fountains. They strolled arm-in-arm along the green-arched aisles of St. James Park. They rode the Underground to the Tower of London and toured its ancient grounds. Shopping at Harrod's and lunch at Ye Olde Cheddar Cheese was followed by a performance of *King Lear* by the Royal Shakespeare Company. True tourists that they were, they even managed to fit in afternoon tea at the Ritz.

Except for the pink shell that awaited them in Laguna and an album of pastel memories, their impressionistic honeymoon days of Hawaii had faded. Now, in a different place and time, they painted their romance with bolder strokes and in richer hues. They talked of everything—no secret emotional shadings were left unexplored. It seemed that a better picture had been roughed out. The lines were clearer, the perspective deeper and more realistic. Perhaps the tears of the past would serve to enliven the colors of the future.

One morning at breakfast, Jon sat reading the morning paper. As usual, Betty was braced for comment about the dead agent. She stirred her tea absently, distracting herself by watching the people that came and went from the old hotel lobby.

"Not a word about that CIA agent in Kiev," he commented.

Lucky for me. "Are you surprised? I wouldn't think the government would be too anxious to see those stories in print."

"I'm sure the CIA wouldn't like it at all, but sometimes gossip gets leaked to the press anyway. No, truthfully I'm not surprised. I have a feeling those kinds of casualties happen more often than we'd care to think."

"So what's new in the paper?"

"Nothing, really. But the same old stuff is really amazing. Do you remember when Charles and Di were married?"

"Of course! It was the wedding of the century. I loved it."

"It's hard to believe that a marriage that started off so beautifully could become such a disaster."

Betty fixed her eyes fondly upon Jon, ever-admiring of his angular face and his clear, blue eyes. He somehow seemed to have grown more commanding since their reunion. More resolute. More confident. Something had changed inside him, and it had empowered him.

"It could happen to anybody, Jon. Their problems just happened to make the papers. That's what always happens to fantasies."

Jon lowered the newspaper and looked at his wife, a serious expression in his eyes. "So you think it could happen to us?"

"Well, I hate to say it, but I think it *did* happen to us. We thought being in love was all we needed and that everything else would take care of itself. We didn't want to talk about our problems or our faults or our weaknesses. We were pretending to be perfect. And, of course, we aren't!"

"What do you mean, we thought love was all we needed? Don't you think being in love is a rather important matter, Betty?"

"Jon, don't be silly. Of course I think it's important. Being in love is the chemistry that makes people want to be together. But life goes on. Whatever kind of people we are, we have to make it work in our daily lives. I guess that's when the wedding march stops and the hard work begins."

Jon was taken aback. Apparently he hadn't thought of the necessary contributions to a successful marriage as "hard work." "Is living with me such a formidable task, then?" he asked with a faint smile.

"Jon," she leaned over and kissed his cheek, "you aren't hard to live with at all! In fact you're wonderful. It's not what you do that I'm talking about. It's the way I react to what you do that causes the trouble. For example, if I assume that you're going to lose interest in me after a while, then I'm going to read that loss of interest into everything you do until it really happens."

"But I'm not going to lose interest in you! I don't understand. Betty, is something bothering you?" By now Jon had dropped the paper and was giving their conversation his full attention. He was obviously distressed by what she was saying.

How did I get into this? I never say things as well as I write them.

"Oh, Jon. Don't look so worried! I'm not upset with you. It's just that I've taken a good look at myself in the past few weeks, and I'm not real excited about everything I've seen. I'm both good and bad. And I'm sure you are too. And when you put two imperfect people together, you're bound to have conflict and confusion."

Jon sat pensively for a few moments. "I guess lovers put each other on a pedestal. They get the idea that the other person is perfect. And so they try to hide their own weaknesses and failures."

"I don't know if we've tried to hide them or not. But as far as I'm concerned, I've been a lot more worried about my weaknesses and failures than I've been about yours.

"Me too," Jon nodded slowly. "I guess, in a way, that's why I went to see Carla's therapist. I knew I'd been at least partly responsible for the problems she and I had, and I was finally ready to listen to all the bad stuff about myself. I thought it might help me be a better husband to you, Betty."

Oh, God. Here we go again. "Jon, I was so wrong to misjudge you."

"I was wrong not to explain."

I might as well say it . . . "You know, Jon. I think the hardest part of being married to you is saying good-bye. I can honestly say that being with you is always wonderful. It's when you're gone that I get into trouble."

"What kind of trouble?"

You don't want to know the answer to that question so don't ask. "Oh, thinking you don't love me. Thinking that if you wanted to be with me, you'd be with me. Of course, Carla's calls didn't help, because I also assumed that you were still romantically interested in her."

They got up to leave the table, and he put his arm around her. "I'm sorry it's hard for you when I'm gone. But it would be pretty hard for me to earn a living without traveling, Betty. Besides, nobody should be together twenty-four hours a day."

"I know that. I just need to change my attitude."

"Speaking of being together twenty-four hours a day, you don't sound like the same independent Betty I heard talking to the Dunns the other night."

"I know. I was just trying to shut her up. I hate being preached at, don't you?"

They walked out the restaurant door into a driving rainstorm. A boat trip down the Thames River was on their sightseeing agenda that day, but according to the newspaper, rain was expected to continue until evening. Jon and Betty decided to go back to their room and reconsider their options. Once they were alone, Jon drew her to himself. "I feel so much closer to you than I've ever felt before," he whispered. "Sometimes talking about things hurts a little, but it's worth it."

After a couple of affectionate hours, which they agreed were the best possible way to spend the rest of a rainy morning, they eventually began to reassess the day's further activities. While Betty perused a London guidebook, Jon decided to call their answering machine at home, ". . . just in case something earthshaking has happened. I haven't checked since I left for Kiev."

He punched in the numbers and codes, listened, and scribbled notes to himself. After a few minutes he glanced at Betty, who was trying to coerce her still-damp hair into some sort of a braid. Jon hung up, staring at her, unconsciously tapping the pen on the bedside table.

"Betty?"

"Hmmm?"

"You're not going to like this."

She turned to face him and recognized that he had a rather odd look on his face.

"I'm not going to like what?"

"I got a call from Dave at *Newsweek* yesterday morning. They know I'm over here somewhere, and they want to know if I'd be willing to fly over to Bosnia-Herzegovina and cover a story there for about three days."

There was a protracted silence, accompanied by unbroken eye contact.

"When?"

"Day after tomorrow."

"Jon, we're supposed to go home day after tomorrow!"

"I know. But maybe you could go on home and maybe I could catch up with you on Sunday."

Betty sat down on the edge of the bed, feeling slightly lightheaded. Jon was still tapping the pen against the table. She didn't know what to say, and she didn't trust her voice anyway. Somehow, the only thought she could identify was Carla's wickedly cackled comment: "So he's still a traveling man? Some things never change."

Jon was persistent. "Should I go home with you or stay? I should call Dave back right away, before it's too late in New York."

"Do we need the money?"

There was another pause, during which Jon considered several points. Sure, they could use the money—they could always use the money. But money wasn't the reason he wanted to go.

"Betty, it's not that. It's just . . ."

She looked at him, waiting for him to finish the sentence. He, perhaps, was waiting for her to finish it for him. He wanted so much to explain himself, but wasn't sure how or whether he would be successful.

Communicate, he told himself. *That's what you failed to do the last time.* "Betty, I'm a photographer, and I love what I do. I get excited when I'm the one who gets the call to cover an important story. I guess I'm the kind of guy who chases fire engines—I like to be where things are happening."

Betty's eyes were starting to fill, and she hated herself for it. *God, I'm wrong to feel this way, but I don't know how to stop.* "Do you miss me when you're gone?"

"Betty, when I have two seconds to think, of course I miss you. And sometimes I'd love to have you with me.

But I guess there's also a part of me that enjoys the freedom and the fact that I'm Jon Surrey-Dixon, and I'm taking the shots for a top news story. It's a part of who I am."

Thanks alot, Jon. So I guess you won't be inviting me along to Bosnia. Right? "I think you should go. It's important to you." Her voice sounded a little cool, although she didn't mean for it to.

"Betty, are you going to be angry?"

"I'm going to go home, put my stuff away, enjoy the beach and look forward to seeing you." *And somehow, I'm going to break this stupid cycle in myself. We're happy. You leave. I'm unhappy. You come back. We're happy again.*

Jon got up, gently took her arm, and pulled her down to sit next to him. "Do you understand what I've been trying to tell you, Betty?"

"I'm trying. I think women are different, Jon. I think a lot of us put the men in our lives ahead of everything else. And part of the problem is that when you're with me, the world just seems happier and friendlier. When you're gone I really feel it—it's sort of like the lights have gone out. Females are like that, I guess. Anyway, you go ahead. I'll deal with myself."

Jon was trying valiantly to speak the truth without causing unnecessary pain. "I learned something about myself from those sessions with Carla and her therapist. When I was married to her, I wasn't honest when I didn't like something she did or said. Instead of confronting her, I would just run away. I'd either run away physically on a trip, or emotionally by shutting her out. I don't want to do that to you, Betty, and I don't want you to do it to me. If you're upset, let's talk about it."

There was more silence, during which Betty thoroughly studied her nails and the backs of her hands.

Finally she answered, "I guess I feel rejected when you leave, Jon."

He nodded. "You're not being rejected. You married me, knowing that I'm a photographer, and that I have to travel. Did you expect me to turn into something else?"

I was kind of hoping you'd get a job at McDonald's. Or, better yet, maybe you could find something to do at the San Clemente car wash. "Jon, it's an emotional reaction, not an intellectual one. Just give me time to work through it, okay?"

He smiled and kissed her on the cheek quite sympathetically. "You've got the rest of your life, sweetheart."

Okay, here goes. Betty summoned every ounce of courage she had left. "Jon? Will you try a little harder to get work close to home whenever you can? And to include me now and then when it's possible? Maybe we can both compromise a little."

Jon watched her as she struggled to speak her mind. He could see that she was valiantly trying not to give in too easily. "That's exactly what I intend to do, Betty. I told you that when we were with the Dunns. I want to be with you, too."

Having completed their conversation quite sincerely, and with every intention of following through on it, Jon was unable to fully disguise his enthusiasm for his new assignment. He quickly picked up the phone and dialed New York City.

"Dave?" he said. "Hi. It's Jon. I got your message. Look, how do you want me to get from London to Bosnia-Herzegovina?"

The following day, in the heart of Westminster Abbey, afternoon light spilled through stained-glass windows, splashing colorful patterns across the bare floor. Big Ben chimed four o'clock as Jon and Betty found their way into

Poets' Corner. It was their last day together in London, and Betty had asked Jon to join her at that sacred site before leaving town.

Gray stone and sedately carved memorials paid tribute to a number of England's greatest poets. Jon watched his wife with pleasure as she traced her finger across some of the beloved names recorded there. He thought of her love of verse and her unique way with words. She, in the meantime, was recalling an earlier trip to the same spot.

Some years before, when she'd been married to Carlton Casey, she had reestablished a friendship with another man—Jerry Baldwin, an old high school acquaintance. Now, back at Poets' Corner, her guilty memories of him reemerged once again.

During a trip to England, she had poured out her most emotional thoughts to Jerry in a stack of letters, trying to include him in every aspect of her adventure. He had never read a word of her literary offerings. Her infatuation with him had ended as abruptly as it had begun, but not before she learned a bitter lesson or two. Even now, she was chagrined, knowing that she hadn't enjoyed her first trip abroad because some ill-chosen "leading man" hadn't been there to share the journey with her.

Jon, who thought her pensive face simply reflected some poetic musing, interrupted her thoughts. Moving his hand in a dramatic, sweeping gesture, he asked, "Shall we make a reservation here for Madame?"

She laughed. "Are you expecting me to drop dead sometime soon? First of all, I'm not English. Second, these guys were great poets. I'm just a hack—you know that."

"You need to show yourself a little more respect. Don't you think it's about time you realized that you're a very talented woman?"

She shrugged off his compliment, uncomfortable with such an optimistic assessment of her gifts. Yet there was something in Jon's words that quietly spoke to her soul. Maybe if she accepted herself as the person she was supposed to be, she wouldn't need Jerry or Mike or Jon—or anyone else—to make the world come alive for her.

Maybe she had never quite learned to appreciate herself as an individual. As a woman. As a writer. As a lover of life.

Maybe it was time she did.

On her first trip to Africa, Betty had traveled there as a single person and had found her autonomy exhilarating. Then she and Jon had fallen in love, and her dependence on him had gradually developed into a craving need. It was high time she readjusted, if for no other reason, because Jon was simply not going to be around all the time. And unless she became content in her solitude, she would either spend her life yearning for him, or she would be back into her old pattern of looking for another man to fill the void.

No more Jerrys. No more Mikes. Never again! I've got to be content by myself.

"Speaking of your poetry, Betty, I want you to write a poem for me while I'm gone. You nearly sent me packing with that last one."

"Oh, you must mean the one I left on the table for you." She smiled as ingenuously as possible. "Sorry about that. But you have to admit it was honest."

"It may have been honest, but it wasn't true."

"It was true as far as I was concerned. But I'll write you another one, Jon, as soon as I forgive you for leaving me again."

Betty was only half-kidding, and Jon responded with half a wry smile. "What am I going to do with you?" He sighed, shaking his head. "I guess all I can do is pray!" He glanced around at the stately old church and at the sparse crowd. Impulsively he took her hand in his. "Why don't you let me pray for you right now?"

His arm around her shoulders, and their backs to the rest of the world, Jon quietly spoke. "Lord, thank You so much for Betty, and for the wonderful gifts You've given to her. I pray that You will help her understand who she is and how valuable those gifts really are.

"Father, Betty grew up feeling ugly and unloved. She wasn't treated warmly at home, and she wasn't taught to believe in herself. She's a different person now, thanks to You, but she hasn't quite learned just how exceptional she really is. I can tell her a thousand times, but unless You help her see the truth, she's always going to feel like a lonely, rejected little girl.

"I pray that You'll put a new heart in Betty, Lord. I pray that You'll give her an inner awareness of her beauty, her talent, and her calling. You know how much she means to me. Give her peace, Lord, that I'll always love her, and that You'll always be with her, even when I'm not.

"Bless us when we're together, and when we're apart, and make our marriage strong. Make Your strength perfect in our weaknesses. Thank You, Lord. In Jesus' name, amen."

The shuttle driver hauled Betty's bags up the stairs to the Laguna Beach apartment, pocketed her one-dollar tip, and left her to carry them inside herself. She smiled as she inhaled the salty breath of the Pacific Ocean, humid and heavy and familiar. One by one she opened the windows. Even before she unpacked, she made herself a cup of coffee and dusted the living room. Then, noticing a couple of small sticks in the firewood box, she kindled a fire and sat quietly in the room, enjoying the solitude.

Her eyes moved across the furniture, and she silently greeted every table, chair, book, and rug. She noticed the pink Hawaiian shell next to the dried flowers, picked it up, and held it tenderly for a moment or two before placing it back on the table. She studied the photograph of herself sitting beneath her Victoria Beach tower, which hung on the wall next to the fireplace. Jon had beautifully framed it with her poem and had presented it to her as his wedding gift.

> Turn our faults into blessings,
> Turn our griefs into praise.
> And for dark hours of sadness
> Give us bright, golden days.

God had been hard at work, answering that prayer. But how lightly she had written it! Never before had she considered the complexity of her request. It was no small feat to turn a fault into a blessing or to transform a grief into praise. As for exchanging a painful life for a happy one, Betty knew that such a thing was conceivable. Her clear, unblemished skin testified of the possibilities. But nothing comes easily—rarely do miracles happen without the travail of fear and doubt and tears.

Even the resurrection was preceded by three days of cruel, hopeless disappointment.

Again her mind wandered back to St. Vladimir's and her revelatory experience there. *Dying, and behold we live*, she thought, remembering the crucifix hidden in her luggage, wrapped up in her dirty laundry.

That same life-and-death principle was at the heart of the matter—dying to self, dying to old ways, dying to disillusionments. Only then could life begin. Only then could that new life begin to bear fruit. Only then could dark hours of sadness be exchanged for bright, golden days.

Impulsively, she dug the crucifix out of the dirty clothes, located a hammer and nail, and hung it opposite the poem, on the other side of the fireplace. "Worthless," the customs inspector had said. It was only worthless if it wasn't understood.

Poor old Daddy. Maybe I'll take it down if he decides to visit us. She smiled, wondering if he'd really told Jon to keep her barefoot and pregnant.

Jon. At long last, the recollection of him came with peace, not with turmoil. At that moment, he was somewhere in the heart of the former nation of Yugoslavia, intently cleaning a lens or changing a roll of film or setting up a shot. Chances were he wasn't thinking about her at all. But eventually he would. And when he did, he would think of her with love.

Meanwhile, she had things to do. She unpacked. She put away her belongings. She telephoned Joyce and Jim and her father and a couple of other friends. She washed clothes. She went to the market and bought a few groceries.

Finally, just before sunset, she walked down the cement stairs to her beach, where she sat at the foot of the tower, spellbound by a quiet procession of waves. The late afternoon was still, the horizon was blanketed with low-lying fog. There were no thundering breakers, no streams of spray flung skyward. Not a sound could be heard on Victoria Beach but the soft splashing of seawater and the far-off drone of a Cessna.

In that time-honored place, Betty usually reflected on her past. Even now, a silent review of characters began to parade through her mind. Betty, the sick child, whose skin stung with pain at the very touch of the salt water. Betty, the lovesick college student, rich in poetry but poor in romance. Then had come the healing and the return to Laguna by the young model Elisabeth, too-quickly married and too-soon disenchanted. There had been divorce and disgrace, and the reemergence of Betty, the writer, and finally the bride of Jon Surrey-Dixon.

Before long, however, Betty's usual set of memories was overtaken by a swirling, shimmering array of colorful new visions. She found herself imagining plots of books she'd like to write—stories of intrigue and romance and wonder. She thought about lands she'd yet to see— "faraway places with strange-sounding names." She fancied houses with rose gardens, atriums filled with flowers, and more bedrooms than she could possibly use. And she thought of children. Was she really thinking of children? Dmitry had kindled a new flame in her heart, and, for the moment, the thought of a family seemed as warming as a winter hearth.

As Betty reflected, a single star began to glimmer between the clouds, high above the silver-green ocean. A song, unheard and untitled, had always played somewhere behind the scenes of Betty's life. It was a symphony of longing, performed in a minor key. Yet, in recent days, it had begun to sound a bit different. It was the same song, yes, but nowadays its chords resolved in peaceful harmony and occasionally even soared, as if in triumph. That evening it sang quietly in her heart.

Would the Elisabeth Surrey-Dixon story have a happy ending? It could. But only if she allowed it to.

Betty got up, placed her palm against the old, stone tower in farewell, and headed toward the apartment.

Later that night, just before she went to bed, she sat at her desk, pen in hand. There was something she wanted to say to Jon. In fact she'd been trying to find a way to express it ever since he'd left her in London.

Once he'd gone, she'd fought off her initial resentment. She'd successfully struggled with her sense of abandonment. She'd ultimately concluded, no matter where he went, no matter how often he left her, that Jon was well worth loving. Jon was Jon, God's best gift to her. And he wasn't likely to change a great deal, one way or the other. Whether she accepted him, for better or for worse, was completely up to her.

"Write me a poem," he had asked her in Poets' Corner. Before she went to bed, quite alone, she began a verse. It would be waiting for him, on the table, when he arrived home on Sunday morning.

> Ever dear and always welcome;
> Far or near, you cannot stray
> From my heart, where I will keep you
> Even when you walk away.
>
> Sunlit heights, alive with angels,
> Depths where demon voices call;
> Days of wonder, nights of sorrow—
> I have loved you through them all.
>
> Still I love you. Still I hear you
> Call my name and calm my fear.
> Bearing hope, your hands are God's hands,
> Always welcome, ever dear.